"YOU DON'T OWN ME. NOT NOW. NOT EVER."

"No one ever owns anyone else," he soothed. "I wasn't talking about ownership and I never would, Cissy. Don't be quarrelsome."

"Me, quarrelsome? What about you? You're the one with the comments that cut me to ribbons."

Incredibly, he laughed. "Cut you to ribbons, do they? I'll have to remember that."

"Don't laugh at me, Desmond. I can't stand that."

He lifted her above him, his hands on her waist, and settled her along his length. "It's either laugh at you or love you. One or the other."

His mood astounded her. "Then you'll have to laugh, I guess," she said. He began stroking her back and pressing her against his body. She drew back to look at him. "You can't—"

"I thought we'd already established that I can. And I do. Now."

"Desmond."

"Make that Des," he said against her mouth.

CANDLELIGHT ECSTASY ROMANCES®

RUN
TO RAPTURE

MARGOT PRINCE

A CANDLELIGHT ECSTASY ROMANCE®

Published by
Dell Publishing Co., Inc.
1 Dag Hammarskjold Plaza
New York, New York 10017

Dell® TM 681510, Dell Publishing Co., Inc.

Candlelight Ecstasy Romance®, 1,203,540, is a registered trademark of
Dell Publishing Co., Inc., New York, New York.

ISBN: 0-440-17521-6

Printed in the United States of America

First printing—August 1984

To Our Readers:

We have been delighted with your enthusiastic response to Candlelight Ecstasy Romances®, and we thank you for the interest you have shown in this exciting series.

In the upcoming months we will continue to present the distinctive, sensuous love stories you have come to expect only from Ecstasy. We look forward to bringing you many more books from your favorite authors and also the very finest work from new authors of contemporary romantic fiction.

As always, we are striving to present the unique, absorbing love stories that you enjoy most—books that are more than ordinary romance.

Your suggestions and comments are always welcome. Please write to us at the address below.

Sincerely,

The Editors
Candlelight Romances
1 Dag Hammarskjold Plaza
New York, New York 10017

CHAPTER ONE

The coffee in the paper cup was cold, but Cissy continued to sip from it, delaying the time she'd have to leave the gymnasium to find Lucky. She sighed and focused her wide hazel eyes on a gaunt gray-haired man doing his stretching routine against the cinderblock wall. His nylon shorts looked new, but instead of the matching mesh singlet most runners wore he had on a tattered Disneyland T-shirt. His lucky shirt, Cissy thought, noting with amusement his inward, yogalike expression as he completed his hamstring stretches and carefully, almost reverently, lifted his left foot behind his buttock to stretch the large quadricep muscle at the front of the thigh.

Runners are a funny lot, she mused, casting her eyes over the teeming room. Her detachment felt odd and more than a bit lonely. She had always been too busy before, too involved, to look outside herself at her fellow athletes. Even after six weeks she wasn't comfortable merely contemplating the scene; she still wanted to be a participant, not an observer.

It was over an hour before race time, yet many runners were beginning to leave for the starting area. All her friends were gone already, and Lucky would be angry if she didn't get to the van soon. Since he wasn't happy with her anyway, she didn't want to irritate him more by being late. She gathered up her crutches and swung her bandaged right leg over the cafeteria-style bench into the aisle behind her. The knee had grown stiff under its wrap while she sat, so getting to her feet was an ungraceful process that sent one crutch crashing behind her. On one foot, she teetered in a stiff half circle to find and pick up the crutch, only to have it placed deftly under her arm while a solid masculine forearm supported her securely around her waist.

Cissy sucked in her breath and looked up beside her into warm brown eyes that laughed down into her startled face. She'd heard, or maybe read, that eyes could laugh, but she'd never believed it, certainly never seen it before. The impact of those eyes—no, she corrected herself quickly—the way he had come up behind her with no warning, made her heart do funny things in her chest.

She looked down at his arm, still around her waist, holding her slight body close to the warmth of his side, and said pointedly, "You can let go now. I'm all right, thank you." She didn't feel all right. She felt alarmed and queasy. The fingers of his large hand were spread over her stomach and rib cage, making it hard for her to breathe. Wildly, she tore her eyes away from the rust-brown hairs curling at his wrist and lightly peppering the backs of each finger. They matched the color of his eyebrows and thick head of hair. It wasn't red, but like her own strawberry-blond hair it had red highlights.

He took his arm away and she sagged onto the crutches, for once grateful for their support.

"Are you going to do the race on crutches?" There was no trace of condescension in his deep voice. The laughter she'd seen in his eyes was gone.

10

"No," she managed, straightening to swing along the informal aisle between the tables. "I'm checking times for . . ."

"I know," his voice interrupted on a rising note, "you're Cissy Barlow. I was just reading about you in the paper."

She had seen the item, a human interest sidebar about how injury had killed her chances of making the Olympics. Newspapers loved stories like hers, dwelling on her disappointment after years of struggle and training. Dashed hopes and broken dreams were almost as good as success for selling papers, but the space given to failure was much smaller.

"You don't look like your picture."

His disconcerting eyes roved her face and body in a way that made her blush. "It's an old picture."

He stood so close, she could feel his influence on the air next to her skin. She wanted to step back, but before she could he took her hair in both hands and lifted it back as if to put it into her trademark hairdo, a French braid at the back of her head. "Yes, now I can see it," he said in a voice so low he seemed to be talking to himself, "that pointed little chin, so determined." He dropped her shoulder-length hair almost reluctantly. "I like your hair better down like this."

Cissy couldn't believe she was standing still for this. She didn't even know his name and already he'd had his arm around her and rearranged her hair. She drew her lapsed dignity and self-possession around her again and stepped back decisively from him.

He got the message and drew himself up also. "I'm sorry. That was rude," he apologized. "That's the trouble with celebrity, isn't it? Just because people know you they think they can make themselves at home with you."

His smile showed dazzling white teeth as he put out his hand for her to shake. She took it reluctantly. It was as warm as she remembered it being on her waist. "I'm Desmond McGinnis. I'm twenty-nine years old and I have all my teeth except for two wisdom teeth that tried to come in sideways. I live in Brookline, I'm an engineer, I'm not married, and I have no children that I know of."

Before Cissy could absorb or react to that speech and before she could get her hand out of his grasp, he asked, "Cissy is a nickname, isn't it? What's your real name?"

She smiled then for the first time. "Mary Elizabeth Rose, would you believe? My brother called me Sis rather than tackle all that, and I just changed the spelling once I got to school and found out what a sissy was." Her smile became an outright laugh. "I've never told a single soul that. Outside my family everyone assumes Cissy is my given name."

"Then I won't tell anyone." He gestured to her knee. "What's the prognosis for your knee?"

"Long term it's good. I won't need surgery, but I won't race again this season."

"That's tough. Are you going to watch the race?"

"I'm clocking at halfway for my coach. Are you with a club?"

"I'm not in your class. I do this just for fun."

Cissy made her way ahead of him to the wide double doors to the outside. She noticed that he paced himself to her precisely, neither hovering nor hurrying her, and she was able to relax almost enough to forget her hated crutches. Outside, he walked along beside her as she headed for the club van, then he stopped. "Cissy, I have to get over to the start. I haven't even picked up my number. I'll look for you at the halfway mark."

She said, "Good luck. It's a good running day."

12

It was. The sky was bright, but there were enough clouds to give relief, and the breeze would gust primarily from behind the runners. She meant to swing off immediately, but he made no move to go and she felt held by something in his eyes as he looked down at her.

"Do you have a good-luck token you always race with?"

His question startled her. "Yes. I'm as superstitious as most runners."

"What is it?"

Instinctively, her hand went to the valley between her breasts. "A lucky sixpence my brother brought me from England."

"Would you let me wear it? I always try to carry all my friends' charms. I'd be sure you get it back safely." From the change pocket at the inside of his shorts he showed her a rabbit's foot and another coin.

Cissy noticed several chains around his neck then and said, "You look well provided with luck already, but, yes, it would be nice to know my sixpence was in the race even if I can't be." She didn't need to undo the slender gold chain to take it off, but it was awkward to hold the crutches and remove the necklace too. In the end he helped free her hair from snagging in the loop and propped one crutch against his chest as she fit it over his head. Her stomach gave a funny little turn as the charm disappeared under his jersey to nestle among the dark chest hair she could see through the thin cloth.

"Do you remember my name?"

"Desmond McGinnis," she repeated in a voice so soft she almost didn't recognize it.

"Good. I'll find you again after the race. Don't drop your crutches on any other man until then, okay?" He touched the end of her nose with his index finger, then he left.

Cissy felt as disoriented as if she had dreamed him and the whole conversation. She even peeked under her jersey to be sure the necklace was really gone. Had she actually given it to him? She laughed out loud and shook her head.

Lucky was waiting by the van, a frown joining his heavy brows into one slash of disapproval across his forehead. Ordinarily his scowl would upset her, but something in her encounter with Desmond McGinnis made her temporarily impervious to Lucky's temper. She felt absurdly happy for the first time in months. She ignored Lucky's mutterings and clambered into the back of the van for the trip to the winding road the racers would follow.

Cissy had never seen a more beautiful race setting. It was a ten kilometer road race, but the course had never been used before for a race because it was within part of the enormous Cape Cod seacoast preserve administered by the federal government. That someone had prevailed on the supervisory agency to permit a one-time race along part of the road to publicize the park and celebrate its anniversary was a minor miracle to Cissy. The just-over-six-mile course was already lined with people, most of whom had obviously made a day of the race judging from the numbers of picnic hampers and beach chairs she could see as they drove the route.

Their first stop was at the end of two miles where a water station had been set up. Lucky had fixed rules about races and every Colonial Club runner would drink water at each of three spots along the course. At the halfway point Cissy would note the exact time to the fraction of a second each runner had taken to get to her.

14

Her companion, Wanda, would give out the water, but not until the racers had passed her magic mark to get their all-important split at 3.1 miles. Lucky's wife, Edna, would give out the last drink, while Lucky posted himself at the point where each runner was to begin her sprint to the finish line. Although the race was for both men and women, all Colonial Club runners were women, hand-picked by Lucky for their talent and dedication. It was a privilege to run for Lucky Edwards, and he never let one of his runners forget it.

Cissy's spot turned out to be at the first crest of a series of three small rises among the dunes with a glorious view of the Altantic Ocean off to her left. Although there was no shade to shelter her from the sun, Cissy approved the location wholeheartedly. She would have time to spot each of the runners she was to time as the flock came up the first rise. The club's distinctive yellow and blue jerseys were always easy to catch, even in a crowded field such as this would be.

An open race in such a lovely setting would naturally attract hordes of joggers as well as many world-class athletes, especially since the distance was vastly more manageable for untrained runners than the grueling twenty-six-mile marathon. As a committed athlete Cissy could understand the lure of racing for joggers, and she enjoyed the feeling of support she got from the vastness of the field behind her in events like this, but Lucky didn't share her generosity of spirit. He wanted more invitational events on the schedule. If he'd had his way, the club would never have come to run here today. He had only been persuaded to commit his runners because of two things—the quality of the field and the timing of the race. He found it hard to resist pitting his club against world-class runners at any time, but timing was the thing that put this race on his calendar with a red star next to it. Superior racing times here would help prepare his athletes for the Olympic trials that would soon follow. And of course Cissy had been his prime contender for a berth on the U. S. Olympic team.

This race was to have been the one where Cissy Barlow made her big move and established herself as a great runner and, incidentally, brought the racing world's attention to her peerless coach, Lucky Edwards.

Cissy looked at the shimmering Atlantic and wondered at her momentary bitterness. She had felt anger and disappointment galore ever since the pain in her right knee had crossed the line between bearable and excrutiating, but, before, the emotions had always been directed at herself. If anything, she'd felt only guilt about Lucky, knowing she had let him down. But today she realized she was also angry with Lucky because he had failed to give her any emotional support after her injury. Admittedly, emotional support wasn't ever his strong point, but he had acted as if she had deliberately injured herself to spite him. Of course, she had sustained the injury while trying out a small variation in her natural gait that she had hoped would improve her final sprint, so there was cause for guilt on her part.

The sprint was her weakness, that all-important final kick that could, done properly, leave the opposition yards behind at the finish line. It had to be done anaerobically, literally without sufficient air, and for that reason it was the part of race preparation most dependent on training methodology for success. Each coach had a pet theory of how sprint training should be accomplished by distance runners, and each theory was sacrosanct to followers of that trainer, supposedly.

But Cissy hadn't improved enough using Lucky's

method, so in her independent way she had searched in the abundant literature of running for a theory she thought might help her. She believed she'd found it, too, until the wracking pain of torn cartilage had told her otherwise.

So now she was on Lucky's hit list. From favored runner to fair game in one searing moment of pain and failure. Her fall from grace was so precipitous and complete, even her friends in the club were afraid of treating her with sympathy lest they invite his wrath upon themselves as well. She was here today only because she had insisted upon coming, and until now she'd begun to believe herself a bit of a masochist for bothering. But, after all, running was her whole life. The women she was about to time were her best friends. Why shouldn't she be here? She was going to recover. She would race again. Not in the Olympics, of course, but that was her personal tragedy, and if she could bear it with hope, why couldn't Lucky at least be civil?

Cissy lifted her pale hair back from her face and turned to the capricious breeze wafting from the water. The gesture reminded her of the man who had done that only an hour ago, and it brought a smile to her mouth. The heat made her wish she'd braided her hair back, but if she had, Desmond McGinnis wouldn't have touched it as he had. Before she let her hair fall again she tried for just a moment to put herself in his shoes and feel its weight as he had. In that small reluctance to let go of her hair he'd somehow communicated an overall attraction he seemed to feel for her and she wondered how he'd managed to do that.

Her hair wasn't remarkable to her. In fact, it's fine texture was a problem for which she'd never found the solution. Braided, it managed to wisp out in little flyaway strands around her face and neck that were her despair. Let free, as now, it still trailed off every which way and blew with every breeze. The color was nice, she knew, strawberry-blond with both pale and red highlights, but even that contributed to a look of innocence she had been tired of at fifteen. At twenty-six she longed for a more sophisticated, worldly image. Certainly her progress up the executive ladder at First Fiduciary of Boston would be aided if she could shake her image as everyone's cute little kid sister.

After a glance at her watch told her it was minutes before the start of the race, she turned her gaze out over the ocean where a bright red sailboat dipped before the breeze, stiffer on the water than here on the side of a protective dune. She cooled herself by imagining she was on board. It helped, but still the major part of her mind was back at the starting line, where she longed to be. She knew the runners would see next to nothing of this beautiful roadway. They might note a dune or the outline of a scrub pine out of the corner of an eye, but every runner's mind would be absorbed by the problems of pace and strategy. *Keep up with the pack, but don't go out too fast.* The motto was engraved in her brain.

The two best runners for the Colonial Club, Allison and Jody, would not be among the first to appear at the halfway point. The best women runners had made great strides toward bridging the gap between male and female runners, but a good male runner could still outperform the best woman in any field. Male physiology—larger, stronger muscles with a lower percentage of body fat— keyed the difference. Because of that performance gap Cissy would not begin timing right away. She could enjoy the first part of the race as that phalanx of great athletes whizzed by at a pace well under five-minute miles.

18

Then she remembered Desmond. She didn't know his number so she couldn't gauge where he would come in the race. He had said he wasn't in her class as a runner, but she still couldn't be sure he wasn't being too modest. He was taller than most of the great runners, with wide shoulders that might hinder his progress, but he had no excess fat and his long legs could counterbalance the drag of his shoulder width and keep him competitive with the mainstream of the field.

Once the first thirty or so, led by the speedster "rabbit" who would pace the leaders but not be one of the winners, had passed her checkpoint, Cissy began to watch for Desmond McGinnis. She was amazed at the clarity of her mental image of him. After all, she'd seen him only briefly, and never at a distance or among others because she had been too rattled and proud to turn and watch him leave. Then, too, his outfit was dark brown and white, not easy to spot among all the blues, reds, and yellows.

As always, police on foot and on motorcycle worked to keep the crowd from narrowing the roadway in their eagerness to see the race. Just as the second team of police swept by her post, Cissy spotted Desmond and gave a whoop of recognition.

"Way to go, Desmond!" she yelled. Then, in a moment of pure insanity, she put her fingers in her mouth and gave a piercing whistle that brought a grin to his face.

He was on her side of the roadbed, and as he neared her place he held out his hand. Startled, she reached for his hand, but it eluded her. Only after he was gone did she remember she hadn't checked his time, but before she could compose herself again and figure out what it might have been she spotted the first of the Colonial Club entrants, Jody, running on the far side of the road, buried in

19

a pack of men. Cissy watched intently for her split and marked it down, already searching for Allison. Once Allison had passed she felt free to relax again, knowing Karen and the others would lag behind this pace. Had she been running, she hoped she would have been dogging Desmond closely.

Thinking of him yet again, she realized he was running freely and well. She didn't really know him, but she knew runners and she could tell by watching him that barring mishap or injury he would finish well ahead of her best time, ahead even of her goal for a personal record. That didn't really surprise her, but she was more than shocked to discover that she felt no resentment that someone who was a self-proclaimed fun runner could so easily outdo her.

She didn't have time to ponder the meaning of that fact before Karen appeared and her time had to be recorded. Karen didn't see her, but the next two did and she gave them encouragement, for both looked tired.

A stout woman next to her took her arm, inquiring, "Is your name Cissy?"

"Yes," she admitted, puzzled.

"Are you the girl one of the runners reached out to? The tall one?"

"Yes."

"Then this is for you. He dropped a piece of paper and my son caught it. I apologize for the fact that he read it, but he didn't notice the name at first. He was curious." She held out a folded paper Cissy took with a bewildered stare.

"Thank you," she said. She tucked it under the clip holding her chart, her curiosity as aroused as the boy's. She didn't attempt to read it until the last Colonial Club runner passed by and was safely recorded, but the boldness of her name in black marker on the paper became the true focus of her attention, not the race.

Unlike most of the audience, she had no interest in watching and cheering on the last half of the participants, so she faded back from the edge of the road in search of privacy. She had no idea what the note would say, but she wanted to get well away from the boy who had read it. Not since fifth grade when John Brady had passed a love note in history class had she felt so foolish.

The note said, "If you can, please stay where you are until my parents and sister can find you and drive you to the finish. Des."

CHAPTER TWO

"So he calls himself Des," Cissy murmured to herself. Bemused, she skimmed it again, trying to read between the lines. He wanted to see her again. Well, of course, he had her sixpence to return, she reminded herself. Even so, she knew he'd asked to wear it, not for luck, but so he'd have a reason to see her again. Which was just fine with her.

But to stay here waiting for his parents to claim her? She had to get to the finish line to give Lucky the charts, not to mention getting to the van for the trip back to Boston. What if they didn't find her? How would they know her? Or she them?

Then she remembered her crutches. They would look for a girl with crutches. Simple. If she didn't wait, though, she had a three-mile trek to make on those very same crutches. Lucky had made no arrangement to pick her up. She hadn't given a thought to getting to the finish line herself, so why would Lucky think of her plight? But Desmond had.

Cissy folded the note again and put it into the pocket of her shorts before she worked her way back farther to sit on a rock by the road. Runners were still passing by, their feet visible through the legs of those watching the race. She had just settled her crutches beside her and eased her knee into a more comfortable position when Wanda broke through the bystanders and flung herself onto the sand beside her.

"I thought maybe you'd started for the finish line," she said. "It's going to be a hellish trip for you. I never even thought of that. Even I'm going to have trouble."

Cissy reached for the thermos of water. "It's okay. I'm going to wait here for a friend. You can take the charts to Lucky. He'll be hot for them right away."

Wanda was nineteen, a college track runner, as Cissy had been, who trained in the summer with Lucky. She had wanted to run this race, but had accepted Lucky's refusal with more grace than Cissy would have in her position. "He isn't very nice to you now. How do you stand it?"

Cissy laughed ruefully. "Not as well as I should. I guess I was spoiled because he was better to me before this. Not great, you understand, but tolerable."

Wanda grinned. "I used to envy you, now I feel sorry for you."

Cissy's smile stiffened. "You shouldn't bother with either emotion. Feelings like that are just a waste of time." Aware that her remarks sounded harsh, she sighed and tried again. "I didn't mean that the way it sounded, really. What I meant was, you have to concentrate on yourself and figure out what you want and how you can get it. My injury will be good for some of the others and maybe for you, so don't get your feelings mixed up with your priorities. In competition you can't afford all that sympathy."

Wanda's expression told her the second explanation hadn't improved the message by much and she smiled again more naturally, in reassurance. "Don't mind me; I only wish I were as tough as I sound."

She believed every word she'd said, though, and perhaps Wanda realized that. It wasn't what she wanted to believe, but it was what experience had taught her. At the bank and in the racing world, sympathy was just so much extra baggage. She still had it, but less and less every day it seemed.

Wanda pushed to her feet and gathered up her belongings. "Do you want more water?" she asked before capping the bottle. "I'll try to get Lucky to drive down and pick you up," she promised.

"Don't bother. My friend has a car. It's okay." She handed up the clipboard.

"We leave by this road anyway, so if you miss your ride we'll find you."

Cissy waved indifferently, suddenly tired. Not to return to the finish line would provoke Lucky's ire, but she didn't care. She would wait for Desmond's family.

She had a lot of time to reconsider her decision, but she didn't change it. She didn't know anything about him really, she told herself even as her mind played back his speech of introduction. But, then, how many men send their parents to follow up on a pick-up? Not many, she would wager.

Cheered by the thought, she rested and enjoyed watching the people around her until even the last of the joggers had passed and people began to mill around. No one was even sure of the winner of the race. Word of mouth back from the finish was characteristically unreliable. Cissy didn't care to find out, not even about who was the first woman, so she stayed seated until she could see cars beginning to nose through the crowd, trying to reclaim the roadway. Then she propped herself on the support of her crutches and waited to be claimed, feeling like a lost piece of luggage. When she realized she was on the wrong side of the roadway to be convenient to cars going toward the finish, she hobbled across to the other side in time to be spotted by a woman with a wide, welcoming smile, waving furiously.

Through the half-open window she called, "Are you Cissy?"

Cissy nodded and hopped a little in place, adjusting her crutches.

"We're the McGinnis family. Won't you get in?" The back door in front of Cissy sprung open invitingly. As Cissy settled into the back awkwardly, hauling the crutches in beside her, Mrs. McGinnis went on. "We were afraid we'd overrun the midpoint. It's not marked. Desmond asked us to bring you with us."

"It's very nice of you," she commented, sinking back. "The air conditioning feels marvelous." Once the plush seat embraced her body in comfort she began to look around, trying to take in impressions of the three people inside without being obvious about it.

"I'm Gwen," the girl beside her said, adding, "the kid sister."

"Cissy Barlow. I'm a kid sister too."

Gwen's smile was remarkably similar to the one Desmond had flashed at her, but her hair was an ashy brown that had none of his redness. Her parents both had gray hair, so tracing the color that way was profitless. Second glance showed Gwen to be older than Cissy had thought, probably seventeen or eighteen. "But I bet you're not kid sister to *four* who are older than you," Gwen complained.

"No. That could be a bit much. I have one brother six years older, but he's enough sometimes." Cissy could see

25

Mr. McGinnis's eyes on her in the rearview mirror, and when she met them, the corners of his eyes crinkled in a smile.

"Richard, you've got to find a way to turn this car around. We'll be all day getting to Des," his wife said.

"That way we won't have as long to wait for him," came his mild reply.

"Did you watch from the finish?" Cissy asked.

"Close to the finish, but it was hard to see much until the first bunch passed. We saw Des though."

"What was his time?"

Gwen told her, "Thirty-one forty-five."

"That's great. If I could do that, I'd be the wonder of the world."

"You already are, my dear," Richard assured her. "I don't know how my son got to meet such a luminary as you, but he's very lucky."

Cissy laughed. "He didn't really have a choice. I dropped my crutches on him. For an athlete, I'm pretty clumsy with them." After she'd said that she wished she'd put it differently. They probably thought she'd done it on purpose as a way to meet Desmond.

Richard McGinnis had turned the big blue Mercury around and silence prevailed as Gwen and her mother peered at the throng, searching for Desmond. Cissy didn't try to help, though she did look idly out the window at the traffic. When she saw the blue and yellow van with the Colonial Club logo on its way past, loaded with her friends and leaving without her, she opened her mouth once in silent protest before she sagged back, resigned. It didn't matter, she thought. She'd get home somehow, even if she had to hitchhike. Then she countered, no, she could take a bus. She'd never dare hitchhike. It would have been nice, though, to have her duffel bag with her. All she had in her small shoulder bag was her wallet, comb, lipstick, and apartment key.

"There he is," Mrs. McGinnis crowed, and suddenly he loomed beside the halted car.

He opened the front door and said, "Give me your keys, Mom, and I'll stick this gear into the trunk."

Cissy had no time to notice him then, because Gwen said to her, "Shove over this way, will you? I'm not having him next to me all sweaty like that. You're a runner, so maybe you don't mind."

"Gwendolyn McGinnis!" her mother remonstrated from the front.

Unoffended, Cissy laughed. "I'm certainly used to it." A thump at the rear of the car announced the deposit of Desmond's bag, and then he was beside her in the car, making the roomy backseat seem cramped. His warm-up suit was brown with gold and white stripes on the chest and down the leg. Suddenly shy and embarrassed to be among a stranger's family, Cissy could only look down the length of his legs and note that he wore Puma's. Big Puma's. She felt the heat radiating from him as before, now coming from the back of her neck as well, for he slid his arm along the back of the seat behind her to accommodate his size to the available space.

"I see they found you," he commented. "Did you wait long?"

"Not really," she dismissed the concern, and shot him a quick glance. "You ran quite a race. Congratulations." Her words sounded stilted to her.

"I was showing off for you," he laughed.

"Nothing like a little inspiration, eh, son?" came his father's amused voice.

"If I'd been running, I'd have tried to catch you. You

27

could have been my personal rabbit and maybe I'd have the world record," she joined in.

"But if you'd been behind me, I wouldn't have been in a hurry."

It was all nonsense, Cissy knew, but the banter helped her feel more comfortable, as it was supposed to.

"Are we going out to dinner tonight?" Gwen asked.

"I have some beef kabobs marinating," Mrs. McGinnis said. "I thought we could grill them on the deck."

"After I get a shower," Desmond added.

"Amen!"

Cissy turned to Gwen and laughed. Desmond touched her arm gently and she turned back to him. "I got your bag from your coach and explained to him that you were coming with me. I hope you don't mind too much."

Before Cissy could respond, his mother spoke up in shocked tones, "Why, Desmond McGinnis, that was high-handed of you! Your note said to kidnap her, but I thought that was just more of your foolishness. Do you mean to say this poor girl hadn't even told you she'd like to come with us?"

"Don't blow a gasket, Mom. If she wants to go back to Boston tonight, I'll take her after dinner. You won't be an accessory to a crime."

Cissy smiled at Mrs. McGinnis. "It's all right. Please, don't be upset."

"It's only about half an hour to the cottage," Desmond said so only she could hear. "Then we'll talk."

Conversation for the rest of the trip was general and easy. The McGinnises asked about her injury and chatted with Desmond about the race until they reached the narrow paved access road to their property. Desmond's description had prepared Cissy for a typical beach house, one of many huddled in a row at the edge of the water, not for this gracious three-story structure of silvery weathered shingles surrounded by deep porches.

"What a lovely house!" Cissy exclaimed.

"We love it," Mrs. McGinnis said. "After next year it will be home year round, but first we have to get Gwen graduated."

The process of getting five people into the house was interrupted by the wild barking of a well-fed Irish setter Gwen released from the house. The dog went straight for Desmond, who put down Cissy's bag to kneel and submit to a thorough face-washing that was impeded only by the dog's need to bark joyously.

"Well, there's my shower taken care of." Desmond laughed, getting to his feet and drying his face ruefully on his sleeve. "Meet Jock," he said to Cissy. "Our trained guard dog. He lies down on the robbers' feet and trips them when they try to leave with our TV."

Once everyone was inside, Desmond steered Cissy to the front porch. "I'll give you the tour later," he said, gesturing to a lounger. Instead, Cissy went to sit on the porch railing and look out across a small sloping lawn to the rocks edging an expanse of sandy brown beach. "Would you like a beer or a Coke? I'm having a beer."

"Whatever you're having will be fine," Cissy answered without taking her eyes off the scenery. She parked her crutches against the post beside her, taking deep draughts of salty air into her lungs. Her eyes were shining when she looked at Desmond to take the offered can of beer.

"I take it I'm forgiven for kidnapping you," he smiled.

"I didn't say that," she hedged.

"I am sorry about that, sort of. I hope I didn't interfere with any plans you had."

"Well, I was going to wash my hair and iron two

29

blouses tonight, but I suppose that can wait till to-morrow."

"Can it wait for Sunday night?"

"I don't know." Cissy looked over the water. "Your family is nice."

"This is only a small part. I have two brothers and another sister."

"All younger?"

"Did Gwen tell you?"

"I guessed. You act like the eldest."

"Bossy, you mean."

She laughed. "Who else has red hair?"

"Mine's not red, but Moira's the real hothead. She's about your age, maybe a little younger. She's married and expecting her first child in a couple of months."

Cissy divided her attention between the view and Desmond, who lounged against the porch support next to her crutches, his eyes intent on her face.

"So tell me about yourself, Freckles," he said softly.

"Damn. You noticed."

"I'm very observant." He drank the beer, still watching her.

"I grew up in Lexington, went to U. Mass at Amherst, and now I have a minute apartment on Beacon Hill and work in a Boston bank. Totally provincial, Massachusetts style."

"But you're a talented runner with world-class potential."

"Past tense now, I'm afraid."

"Injuries are tough, but they don't change talent."

Cissy didn't comment.

"Think about staying the weekend, Mary Elizabeth Rose."

That got her attention. "You said you wouldn't tell!"

"I can tell you. You already know." He was enjoying her indignation.

Cissy tried to will the color from her face. She took a drink, but it didn't help, especially when he laughed.

"You have more red in your hair than I have," he teased.

"You got yours from your mother, right?"

"Guess again."

"Really? But your father's so easy-going."

"Mom's in charge of sweating the little stuff. He saves himself, but then watch out."

"And you take after him."

"I think it's time I showed you to your room and got my shower."

Cissy laughed and gathered her crutches to follow. On the way to the stairs he gave her the layout of the house and made a detour to the kitchen to return their beer cans.

"You'll be in Moira's bedroom," he explained, opening the door to a bright, feminine room with a kelly green rug. "We're a bit Irish, you may have noticed." He went to indicate the closet door and her duffel bag. "We're also pretty informal here, so don't worry about clothes. Gwen will be down to see you in a while. She has the upstairs as a loft for her gang of friends."

He opened another door. "This will be your bathroom. It opens into Kevin's room, but no one is there now. You might want to use the whirlpool in the tub."

Cissy followed to the doorway. "Oh, wow! Paradise."

He gave her a short course in its operation and locked the other door. "Can you rewrap the bandage? I'm pretty handy that way if you need help later. Gwen can let me know. We won't eat for an hour, but feel free to come down anytime."

When Desmond was gone Cissy took her duffel bag to the bathroom and filled the tub, eager to let the whirlpool take away the residual ache a day on her feet left behind. She rested her head against the back of the tub and drifted between waking and sleeping until she heard a knock at the bathroom door.

"Cissy? It's me, Gwen. I brought you some clothes to try on. Des said you might not have a change with you."

"Come on in, Gwen." She began to rouse herself. "I guess I fell asleep. This feels heavenly."

Gwen stood in the doorway a second, then put the clothes on a chair. "I hope you wear a bathing suit sometime while you're here," she said pointedly. "I want to watch Des when he sees you. I wish I had a bosom like that."

"It's no advantage to a runner, I can tell you." Cissy's attitude toward her body was intensely pragmatic. It was the instrument that enabled her to run, nothing more. She began to climb out of the tub, accepting Gwen's hand to steady her and hopping a little on her left leg to reach the towel.

Gwen was an inch or so taller than Cissy and every bit as slender, with a coltish grace that revealed her age as clearly as did her refreshingly blunt manner. She aided Cissy with her underclothes with a tactful simplicity that reminded Cissy of her brother. Maybe it was an inherited trait, this perfect helpfulness, she thought, which would explain why so few people knew how to be helpful to someone with a handicap. It wasn't lack of good intentions with most people, Cissy had discovered since her injury; it was something else she couldn't yet name.

"We don't dress up here, so if you're comfortable with shorts, you'll be fine." Gwen wore jeans.

"They're pretty sad. I'll rinse them out with my underwear before bed. They're nylon, so they'll be ready again by morning."

"Oh, good. That means you'll stay, doesn't it?"

Cissy laughed. "I guess it does. Actually, I don't think you could make me leave here now. You're all so nice to me."

"Just watch out for Des. He's a real heartbreaker."

The warning was given so lightly, Cissy's hand faltered only for a second as she settled a sea green knit jersey over her torso. "Why do you say that?" She made her question as light as she could.

Instantly Gwen began to backtrack. "I shouldn't have said that. He's really a great guy. It's just that girls fall all over him. They all want to marry him."

"But he doesn't want to get married?"

"Oh, he does. Mom says he's waiting for someone special." She passed Cissy an off-white wrap skirt consisting of two tiers of ruffles. It wasn't a style Cissy had ever worn, but when it was tied in place Gwen proclaimed it perfect and she couldn't disagree. "In that jersey your eyes look green, and I thought they were brown."

"My mother calls them hazel, whatever that is."

"Do you want to rewrap your knee? I can help maybe, though Des would do a better job."

"I think I'll leave the bandage off. It feels so good now. It's really just for support, especially when I'm on my feet a lot. I can bear weight on it now sometimes."

"That's great. You must be eager to get back to running."

Cissy didn't comment. The assumption Gwen made was the one everyone made, but lately Cissy had begun to question its truth. She ought to be eager to run, she believed. She sometimes felt lost without the discipline that had framed her life for ten years, but she also felt a liberating sense of ease she'd never really known before. She bent to fasten the sandals she had stuck into her bag on an impulse along with the change of underwear she always carried, glad to have them. She smiled at Gwen and said, "Actually, I think maybe I'm malingering a bit these days. If I worked at it, I could probably do pretty well without the crutches for part of the day."

"Do you want to try it? I could help you."

"No, I don't think so."

"You'd better not let Des know you're not trying to recover. He'd really get after you."

"Who said I wasn't trying to recover?" she countered with a grin.

"Your secret is safe with me," Gwen promised, opening the door to the hallway. Then she laughed. "Well, well, speak of the devil." She scooted past Desmond, saying to Cissy, "I'll leave you to your keeper."

He watched her go. "Whatever she told you, it's not true."

Cissy smiled mysteriously. "Kid sisters have a way of being right on target. Just ask my brother's wife if everything I told her about him didn't turn out to be true. Of course, she didn't believe me then, but I bet now she wishes she had."

He remained in the doorway, looking handsome in khaki pants and gold Lacoste shirt. "I see I'm too late to help you out of the tub."

"You are, but you can help me down the stairs."

"Oh, no, that's good exercise for you. I only do the fun things."

"Gwen was right, I see." She picked up her crutches with a sigh and followed him to the stairs. With him beside her she felt less awkward than usual. Since her injury, stairs had become her bane. Their mere presence before her always made her see herself tumbling down their length in a rattle of crutches and bones.

When she was at the bottom, he asked, "Are you sure you're really an athlete?"

She let out her breath in a stream of resentment. "No, I'm not sure. A psychologist would have a field day with me. Is there some form of symbolism in crutches?"

He didn't smile, but his eyes glinted with amusement. "Probably."

As they approached the kitchen door the hopeful thump of Jock's tail against the floor greeted them. Desmond warned, "Stay, Jock," explaining, "He feels cheated. Being allowed in the kitchen is supposed to be nirvana, but not when the food is on the porch."

"Poor Jock," she sympathized.

"Fat Jock, you mean."

"Don't you take him running with you?" They worked their way to the porch.

"I'm not here enough now, but I used to. He used to be fit, but he got hit by a postal truck and when his injury was healed he'd lost the urge. Now he goes with me only about three houses before he heads back to his chow dish."

"Why do I feel I'm hearing a cautionary tale?"

Desmond's booming laugh announced their appearance on the porch, attracting all eyes.

"You look lovely, dear," Mrs. McGinnis caroled in greeting.

"I hardly ever get to wear such feminine garb. At work I have my little success suits, and the rest of the time I'm in track clothes. This is a welcome change."

"Do they really make women wear those dreary suits?"

"Oh, yes. Mr. Pritchard wouldn't know what to do

with me if I had a dress on. The point of it all is to let people like him pretend I'm not different from the man in pinstripes."

"I think it's silly," Gwen announced.

"What do you do at the bank?" Richard asked from the grill.

"I process loans most of the time. Sometimes I even get to tell a nice young couple why they don't qualify for a mortgage."

"Do you like it?" Desmond asked.

"Sometimes. I'm not really even a full-time employee. It's a management training program that gives me time to train as an athlete. The bank sponsors me, in a sense."

"Isn't that unusual?"

"A bit. It's one of the advantages of being affiliated with Lucky. He has a lot of clout." She took the glass Desmond brought her and tasted it. He watched her reaction. She drank again. "Marvelous," she said.

"Drink it slowly. It may be too strong."

She lifted her chin defiantly. "It's fine."

Desmond laughed and sat near her. She moved away from him a bit. His hand rested lightly on her shoulder. "Relax," he said in that low tone no one else could catch. "I don't bite."

Cissy straightened her back and gave him a frosty smile. "But I do," she said the same way.

His eyes laughed again. "Good."

CHAPTER THREE

Cissy and Gwen, duly annointed with lotion, snoozed away the following morning on towels at the edge of the wet sand above the tideline. They were within sight of the house, and aware, in spite of their somnolence, of Desmond and Jock starting off on a run, and of Mrs. McGinnis, whose husband called her Patsy, lingering over coffee on the porch. They tried to guess how long it would take for Jock to tire and turn back, but they fell asleep before they could find out.

Cissy tried to rouse herself when she heard Gwen called to the house for a phone call, but it took Desmond dripping cold water, drop by drop on her back, to break through her torpor. When she rolled over quickly to escape, she was thankful she hadn't unhooked the back of the bright yellow bikini Gwen had provided. Looking up, she understood what Gwen meant by wanting to see his reaction to her in a bathing suit. Fortunately Gwen missed it.

"That's mean," she protested, sitting up.

"It's an ancient Irish method of torture." He took over Gwen's towel to sit on.

"I thought Indians did it."

37

"They learned it from the Irish." He wore dark brown trunks that enhanced the deep copper brown of his tanned skin. The sun picked out the burnished red of his hair, making even his arms and legs seem to glow. Cissy noticed the absence of the assorted chains, including her own contribution that he'd worn for the race, but what really drew her eye was the deeply muscled breadth of his chest and shoulders. Yesterday he had proved himself as a runner, but unlike most of that breed, he was not whippet-thin.

To cover the fact that she had been staring silently at him for longer than was courteous, she said, "You don't look as if you're suffering any ill effects from the race."

"I was a bit stiff this morning, but my little jog got rid of that. How's your knee?"

"It's having a strenuous day so far, a little whirlpool and a lot of sun. It can't complain."

"Then let's walk it a while and then have a swim."

"I didn't bring my crutches."

"You won't need them." He pulled her up so her right hip rested against the top of his thigh and clamped his left hand in support at her waist.

Stung by the intimacy, Cissy tried to pull back. "We can't walk like this."

"Sure we can." He began to prove it.

"Desmond, this is a public beach."

"Actually, it's not. Dad owns this and we could walk naked here if we wanted to."

"But your mother . . ."

"Is inside fixing lunch, and even if she weren't, she'd know I was helping you walk. She knows how self-sacrificing I am."

His hand slid caressingly over the side of her bare hip and waist to rest for a moment on her rib cage. If it had not been her injured knee near him, she would have tripped him. As it was, all she could do was dig her nails into the side of his waist.

His reaction was a laugh. "Ah-ha! Claws as well as teeth. It gets better and better."

Cissy stopped walking. "You're impossible!"

He swung around to face her and pulled her against him. The top of her head would have fit under his chin if he hadn't tipped her face up with the hand that wasn't holding her lower body close. He had kissed her good night last night, but Cissy knew that had been a mere dress rehearsal for this kiss. His thumb and forefinger held her chin immobile; his fingers splayed over her throat as his mouth descended to hers.

It seemed to take hours for his lips to reach hers. She had the feeling of being underwater, of moving in another dimension, where time had been slowed and stretched beyond bearing, yet with all that time she couldn't manage to turn her face away. His lips were firm and warm, their touch just light enough that she found herself stretching upward, kissing him back as if the whole thing had been her idea. His hand slid to her shoulder, finally ending the kiss, but also reminding her of their near-nakedness and the proximity of his hand to her breast.

She fell back onto her heels and snatched her arms from around his waist, trying to move back. "You did that on purpose," she accused foolishly.

He smiled. "Which *that* do you mean?"

Stupidly, she tried to explain. "The way you kissed me. Just that little bit too gently, so I'd kiss you back." Too late, she saw the trap she'd built for herself.

His chuckle traveled her body like flame along a fuse, but again he postponed the inevitable explosion. "So you'd like a less gentle kiss, eh?" He drew her close

39

again, watching her face, then putting his mouth next to her ear. "What's the opposite of gentle? Rough? Hard?" He kissed along her cheek in search of her mouth. "Why don't you show me?"

"You're doing it again," she said weakly.

By the time he kissed her again she was so hungry for the feeling of his mouth she almost cried aloud with pleasure. The fiery explosion seemed more consuming for having been delayed. She wrapped her arms tightly around his back, reaching for his shoulders. Her hands had a life of their own as they pressed his back, stroking and rubbing the warm smooth skin.

As she had known it would be, this time the pressure of his mouth was exactly right, firm but coaxing, leading her to soften against him in the kind of surrender that felt like victory. She felt the hair that covered his legs and chest, gloried in the heat of his body, and—for the first time in her life—clung to a man spinelessly, not even aware of her surroundings.

Vaguely, from far in the distance, she heard a sound that made Desmond stiffen briefly before he tightened his hold on her in an effort to deny the interruption. Without will, without thought, she parted her lips to his suddenly demanding tongue, allowing, no, welcoming, his invasion of her mouth. It was brief, much too brief, and then she was standing by herself. Desmond's hands supported her shoulders, but he did it to put space between them. Reluctantly, she opened her eyes and blushed furiously. She wouldn't have believed her face could get hotter than it had been, but obviously there was a lot she didn't know about herself.

Confused, she couldn't keep from searching his face for a clue about what had happened, but his face was an unreadable mask. His eyes were dark and every bit as curious as her own. She gave a shaky laugh and took a step backward. "Well, you seem to have gotten the idea very nicely."

Desmond threw back his head in a hearty laugh that, after a moment of disquiet, she joined self-consciously. He pulled her into a quick, hard hug, then scooped her into his arms to carry her back the way they had come. From her new vantage point she could feel his laughter die back to a smile that left his eyes crinkled, reminding her of his father.

"I could walk, you know," she protested, trying to put conviction into her voice.

"Sure you could, but that cowbell meant lunch." He put her down on the porch, adding softly, "This way I have an excuse for my red face." When she blushed he laughed.

"That was mean," she said.

Gwen handed Desmond a tray of sandwiches for the porch table and gave Cissy a merry, "I warned you!" while tactfully guiding her to a powder room off the hall for a much needed respite from everyone's attention.

By the time she felt pulled together enough to rejoin the family she was able to do so inconspicuously. Nevertheless, she was strangely self-conscious about wearing a bathing suit, even with Desmond and Gwen similarly dressed. All her matter-of-fact acceptance of her body seemed to disappear around Desmond. He certainly didn't ogle, but she felt his awareness of her as tangibly as the sea breeze playing over her skin. Although the sandwiches were hearty and delicious, she ate with more doggedness than appetite. Content to let the conversation flow over and around her, she came alert when Patsy told Desmond he and Cissy could have their tickets to a sum-

41

mer stock production of *The Sound of Music* if they hadn't other plans for the evening.

He sent her an inquiring look. "How about it? Are you up to an evening of lederhosen and yodels?"

She couldn't help laughing. "But you shouldn't give up your entertainment for us," she said to the McGinnises.

"They were charity tickets and they'll go to waste if you don't use them. We have plans for a special party with friends," Patsy assured her, adding to Desmond, "We have reservations for dinner, too, unless you want to do your own thing in the kitchen or elsewhere." She looked at her watch and smiled. "The cook here goes off duty in exactly fifteen minutes."

Gwen spoke up quickly, cutting off Cissy's only objection before she disappeared upstairs. "I have something you can wear. I'll put it in your room before I leave. Have fun."

Cissy got up to help with the clean-up. But since that was largely a matter of disposing of paper plates and cups, Desmond quickly reclaimed her, announcing it was time for her to swim.

"But I just ate."

"You'll be in no danger of drowning. This is therapy."

And it was. But for Cissy's awareness of Desmond's hands and his disconcerting nearness, she would have thought she was at the rehab center. The water was only cool enough to keep her alert.

Distracted by his supporting hand under the back of her waist, she failed to respond to one of his commands and got squirted by a small jet of water he squeezed at her.

"How do you know all this?" she demanded, righting herself in the waist-high water.

"I have many talents," he answered evasively. "Now, do what I say."

"Not till you explain all this."

"Finish now and I'll tell you later. Over dinner, if you behave."

"What kind of an engineer are you anyway?" she persisted.

"Mechanical."

His expression was as adamant as hers, so she gave in, but not without warning him, "I'm not going to forget, you know. I'm very persistent."

"I know."

"But you don't know *me*. Don't think you do."

Desmond smiled with irritating complaisance. "Whatever you say. Now, float on your back again or I'll duck you."

She complied slowly, screening her reluctance with another question. "Why is the water so warm this early?" It was late June.

"The Gulf Stream goes by this side of the cape."

"What town is this anyway?"

His patience was being taxed. Very slowly he began her name, "Mary . . . Elizabeth . . ."

"I didn't know there was a town named that," she said innocently, beginning the kicks he had ordered, and just in time she was sure from his expression.

She walked easily from the water to the towels that were still where she and Gwen had left them. Once down on the sand, she had every intention of continuing the sunbath Desmond had interrupted earlier, but he rolled her over to face him.

"You've had enough sun for one day. If you want a nap, do it upstairs."

Cissy took a deep, calming breath that still didn't disguise her burgeoning resentment. "Look, Desmond, I'm not a two-year-old."

"Then don't act like one," he responded. "You know I'm right. Your skin is far too fair for this much exposure."

"That's why there are sun screens," she countered, reaching for the tube.

"But you weren't even going to put any on."

Her smile was saccharine. "I thought you'd do that."

His eyes measured her. He took no deep breath as she had done, but she wasn't fooled by the deliberately conversational tone he adopted to say, "It's been at least two years since I've exercised my temper, Cissy, so why don't you just come along gracefully and let me keep it that way?"

Her glare was long and hard, but finally she got to her feet. She told herself she was only getting up so he couldn't intimidate her by his physical size, but that excuse lasted only until he stood too. In no way could her acquiescence be termed graceful.

Her relief was disproportionately huge when he broke their glaring match by bending to gather up the towels, putting them into Gwen's beach bag. She made no move to help and even tried to shake off his assistance up the slope to the house.

"Don't worry. You'll get used to it."

Cissy flung off his hand and turned to face him, angered by the hint of amusement she had heard. "It isn't funny, Desmond. I'm tired of people pulling my strings because they know what's best for me. I'm twenty-six years old and I make my own decisions, my own mistakes!"

"The way you did with your knee?"

"Yes, damn it! I'm beginning to think it's the best thing that ever happened to me."

"You may be right." His tone was entirely serious and the look in his eyes was even admiring, but then he reverted to the form she had come to expect from him. "But tonight I'd rather dine on lobster than escort one to dinner."

Her pride mollified somewhat by that moment of acceptance, Cissy was able to laugh and concede.

Once she was in Moira's lovely room, showered and shampooed, with her hair blown dry, she knew his insistence had kept her from an uncomfortable, if not serious, burn. Her delicate ivory skin tanned reluctantly, achieving only a peachy glow that faded within a week if not reinforced assiduously. She couldn't help envying Desmond's deep rich color and the ease it gave him outdoors.

She turned back the green lattice-printed bedspread and crawled between cool sheets without bothering to find the T-shirt she'd worn last night as a nightgown. She had intended to ponder the enigma of Desmond McGinnis and figure out what was happening between them, but within seconds she was asleep.

She wasn't aware of dreaming about him, but when she sensed his presence at the side of the bed he was such a natural extension of her thoughts that she could find no surprise in herself. She stayed very still; only her eyelids moved, her lashes like indolent fans in the warmth of the room.

"I did knock. Several times." He sat on the mattress without touching any part of her slight body.

Cissy wanted to stretch, or at least move, but she was so conscious of her nakedness under the sheet she didn't dare. "I was asleep."

"That seems to be another of your talents."

"It's so restful here." A small movement betrayed her, and she saw his knowing smile.

"It's all right. You can move. Tempting as you are, you're quite safe, you know."

She let out her breath slowly. Was she so transparent he could read her every thought? Piqued, she lifted her arms over her head and gave in to a catlike stretch. The sheet stayed in place, thanks to the way she wiggled lower at the precise moment she arched her back slightly against the bed. His attention to every nuance of her move was unnerving. "Of course I'm safe," she said lightly. "After all, your parents are just downstairs."

"I'll be interested to see if you'll stretch and wiggle that way again when you realize that we're quite alone here."

Her surprise threatened the sheet more than her stretch had. She clutched it with both hands, uncaring that he laughed.

"I can see you're a special category of tease, one as yellow as your hair."

Stung, she sat up to face him, keeping a death grip on the sheet. "I am not a tease. And I certainly didn't ask you to come in here."

Silently, he took in the pallor of her face for several seconds before he got to his feet. "No offense meant, Cissy." He made no attempt to hide the fact that he recognized he'd scored a direct, if unintended, hit on some still-raw nerve. "We should be leaving in a half hour or so. Will that give you enough time to get ready?"

She didn't trust her voice to answer, so she nodded. It was so obvious she had overreacted to his remark that she wanted to apologize. When he was gone she flung herself back onto the bed. When, oh, when, would she ever get it right. She moaned to herself. She had finally met a man she really liked, who seemed to like her and find her attractive, and she was well on her way to ruining everything. What *everything* was, she wasn't ready to acknowledge, but its ruin was as real to her as the room.

In need of activity, she threw back the sheet and went into the bathroom. She didn't need another shower, but she took one anyway just to erase the pinched and mottled look left by the battle her emotions had fought with her beginning suntan. When she was dressed in lacy bikinis and bra she realized she had no idea what Gwen had picked out for her to wear. She found it on a hanger on the closet door, a sundress of apricot taffeta that rustled when she touched it. A flounce of ruffles edged the skirt, and as she looked for a way to try it on she saw that it was another wrap-and-tie design that would fit her perfectly. Narrow spaghetti straps were meant to tie at the neck, halter style, making it impossible to wear her bra.

Cissy couldn't contain her delight as she made the ties secure and felt the sensuous material embrace her slim waist. The artful tucks emphasized her full breasts, while the flare of the skirt made her athletic legs look impossibly long and feminine. She had no jewelry except the simple gold hoops she had worn in her ears all week, but the warm color of the dress made her shoulders seem ornament enough. She decided to wear her hair down loose at the back, but pulled back from her face into gold clips that looked a bit more formal.

Satisfied with her appearance, she worked her way carefully down the stairs by holding onto the bannister. She simply would not spoil the look of her dress by using crutches. Absorbed in the struggle to navigate the stairs, she didn't see Desmond looking up from the hall.

Her awkwardness appealed to him deeply. He wanted

47

to pick her up and carry her wherever she wanted to go. At the same time, he admired the independence and determination that was as much a part of her as her fragile beauty. From the moment his arm had first gone around her slender frame he'd wanted to keep her at his side. Even at rest, her body was compressed motion, a coiled spring poised to fling her away from him. His instinctive reaction to that was to tighten his hold and prevent her from leaving, even at cost to her dignity and perhaps his own. But he knew it wouldn't work. She wouldn't permit it.

So he watched and waited until she wouldn't be harmed if his sudden appearance startled her. He took her hand at the foot of the stairs and kissed her cheek. "You look lovely, Cissy."

At his words some of the uncertainty in her eyes eased. "It's the dress. I've never worn anything so pretty."

"The dress is pretty, but you make the dress, not the other way around."

"You look pretty handsome yourself." His lightweight dark brown suit skimmed his body, hinting at the lean muscles of chest, shoulders, and thighs underneath. His white shirt contrasted with the tan of his skin and emphasized the flash of his eyes and teeth as he talked. Even Mr. Pritchard couldn't fault his correct, striped tie, but no one she'd seen at the bank could approximate the rakish air he gave to the assembled costume.

Desmond wasn't strictly handsome, Cissy decided as she watched him drive. His face was strong and full of character, his nose straight and a bit harsh, like his jawline. But the severity of those features was more than offset by the humor of his mouth and eyes. Humor and a sense of perspective seemed to protect him from that deadly seriousness that plagued other men, particularly in the business world her father and brother inhabited.

It was probably that sense of humor that had kept his temper in check for over two years. She wondered what had caused the last flare. Probably something of greater importance than her small rebellion on the beach, she decided. On the other hand, if she could make him blow his carefully nurtured cool simply by resisting one of his directives, they could be in for a rough time. It wasn't a thought that gave her pleasure.

"Do you live alone, Cissy?"

The question startled her from her reverie. "No. I have a roommate. In fact, she had the apartment first. I replaced a friend of hers who got married." She looked over at him again. "Why do you ask?"

"It just occurred to me you didn't let anyone know you'd be staying here. Doesn't anyone keep track of you?"

"Does anyone keep track of you?"

"My parents do, sort of."

"You mean in my shoes you'd have called your parents to tell them where you were staying?"

"I might have."

"Pardon me if I don't believe that."

He laughed. "Okay, I guess it was a sexist question. It's just that you seem so vulnerable to me I can't help being concerned."

"That's only because I'm on crutches now. Normally I don't seem that way."

He swept her with a glance. "How little you know about the way you appear."

"You just haven't seen me with my briefcase and my scarf that looks like a tie at the neck of my suit."

"You'd look like a twelve-year-old playing dress-up."

She worked to keep her voice even. "You really know how to build up a woman's self-esteem, Desmond."

He laughed. "You don't consider that a compliment, do you?"

"Would you like to be compared to a little boy?"

"But I'm not a girl."

"Woman," she corrected him. "I may look younger than I am. I may not be six feet tall. I may even giggle sometimes. But I'm not a girl anymore. I'm intelligent and I work hard. I don't want to be condescended to."

He sighed. "Point taken. Can we erase my comments from the record?"

"You're really a lawyer."

"Dad is."

"Really? Everything you've told me about him so far surprises me."

"He's a surprising man. You'd be shocked to see him in a courtroom. He's all histrionics. I couldn't believe it the first time I saw him. He doesn't do much trial work now, but in his prime you would have said the stage lost a great actor. He turns it on and off like a faucet."

"Better that than never turning off the public persona, wouldn't you say?" It seemed a mild comment to Cissy, but she wasn't aware of the edge to her voice.

"What does your father do?"

"He's in business. Have you heard of Barlow Security Systems?"

"Locks?"

"The works. Everything but guard dogs and mine fields to protect private property."

"You don't approve?" Desmond asked.

Cissy tried to think how to explain her lack of enthusiasm. "It's a fine business, but any obsession wears out people who don't share it. Let's just say I'd have been happy to find the Off button on my father years ago."

Desmond laughed easily. "If she's like my mother, your mother probably manages his switches without him even knowing it."

The remark interrupted a cynical laugh from Cissy, making her thankful their arrival at the restaurant precluded further questions from Desmond. But once the amenities of ordering and being served were out of the way he picked up his line of questioning as if the interruption had never happened.

"Are your parents divorced, Cissy?"

The question surprised her. "No, as far as I can tell, they're entirely happy with each other."

"But you don't think they ought to be happy."

"Of course they ought to be happy," she argued. She was being dense, trying to keep him off course. He was entirely too perceptive for her comfort.

He shook his head. "Does your father have affairs? Or your mother?"

"Really, Desmond, you're being absurd," she protested.

"Not absurd, unfortunately, but rude, undoubtedly."

"The stage may have lost an actor in your father, but the courts certainly lost a lawyer in you."

"If you volunteered any information about yourself, I wouldn't have to put you on the stand this way."

"Why should I volunteer information?"

"Most women do."

"I'm not most women." She could sense his irritation growing. She batted her lashes at him mockingly. "If I want to be a woman of mystery, you should indulge me."

51

That ploy did nothing, so she was direct. "You're only angry with me because you feel in the wrong. You know all this probing isn't polite."

His sense of humor saved the situation. He saluted her with his wineglass.

Cissy spent several seconds buttering a roll before she spoke again. "Besides, there isn't any mystery. My parents *are* happily married. In fact they have exactly the kind of marriage a chauvinist like you would approve of."

"Ah-ha! Then that's why you don't approve."

"Maybe so. I can't explain it. Anyway, it doesn't matter what I think. It's what they think and feel that counts."

"So it is. But you do think and feel, too, and that's what counts with me. My probing, as you call it, was uncalled for, except for that reason."

"How can you say that? You don't even know me."

"You keep saying that. Of course I don't know you. Yet. But I want to know you, so trying to keep me at a distance isn't going to save you. I'm just as determined as you are. In fact, all your deviousness only makes me more determined."

"I'm not devious."

"Not consciously, perhaps, but you seem to try for an inordinate amount of control."

"Don't you? Do you wear your heart on your sleeve?"

"Pretty much, I'd say. I'm an extrovert."

"Which means you hide behind a smokescreen of surface charm," she said flatly.

"Surface charm! Woman, you wound me. This charm goes all the way through me."

She laughed. "See? Pure blarney!"

He laughed with her, but his eyes were serious. He shook his head at her sadly. "Just my luck. I have to meet a pink and gold steel marshmallow."

CHAPTER FOUR

No man had ever described her in those exact words before, Cissy thought, probably because few men were as glib as Desmond. She knew there was a certain validity to the assessment, and it was phrased more attractively than other terms she'd heard. Nevertheless, she was unprepared for the almost visceral pain his words inflicted. It took every bit of power she possessed not to flinch.

"Strength is as important to a woman as to a man," she told him evenly. Hoping to counter any betraying tremble she was afraid he would see, she lifted her chin. "I can't help the way I look. . . ."

"Why would you want to?"

"Maybe I don't like marshmallows."

"But I do."

"I don't think you really do. It's a pejorative term."

"Something like 'surface charm'?" His left eyebrow cocked at her humorously.

"How can I duel with you properly when you keep making me laugh?" she demanded, doing just that.

"That's another Irish trick. But don't worry, I'll wear the scars from this duel a long time."

Cissy watched as Desmond picked the meat out of a

large lobster claw. Even wearing the restaurant's protective bib he didn't look silly. She toyed with her glass of white wine for a minute before she said, "I don't want to pick another fight with you, Desmond, but you did promise you'd tell me about your job."

"Well, I'm an engineer. I design mechanical things that somebody else builds before they're tested out. Does that sound fascinating?"

"I'm sure it's a lot more interesting than you're trying to make it sound. Is that because you think I wouldn't be able to understand?"

Desmond put down the pick he'd been using and searched her face with his eyes. "Do you always see the possibility of a hidden insult in what people say to you?"

"Not usually. I just sense an evasiveness about you. I don't think I believe you're really an engineer. I've known a few of them, and you're nothing like the ones I've met." She began to giggle as one particular date she'd had came to mind. Desmond smiled, encouraging her to share the joke.

"I'm not laughing at you, just at a date I had years ago with an engineer to go to the beach and out to dinner. He lectured the whole day. About why the sand under your feet dribbles away faster and faster when a wave ebbs around you. About the surface tension in a cup of coffee and why the little bubbles gather into clumps on the top. It was unbelievable. I've never forgotten him."

"Now you tell me how to become memorable," he said with a mocking moan. "Maybe I should have boned up on some physical principles to dazzle you with."

"If you were a real engineer, you wouldn't have to bone up. You'd know them," she said severely.

"I'm real enough, but unlike your friend I learned a

long time ago that nonengineers find technical things boring, and that includes my specialty too."

"Which is?"

"If I said seduction, would you believe me?"

"I'd believe you, but I wouldn't believe you think it's boring."

"It isn't to me. I never said it was to me."

She tried a different tack. "How do you know so much about physical therapy?"

"It's the major technique I use to seduce a woman. Whirlpools are irresistible."

Cissy was finding her annoyance growing. "Be serious, Desmond."

His gaze wandered over her bare shoulders. "Oh, but I am serious," he said softly.

In spite of her irritation, the way he looked at her was having an effect she tried to counter by giving her attention to her scallops. But they didn't require much of her, and her eyes crept back to his face. He still watched her with laughter lurking behind something in his eyes she couldn't quite name. "You really aren't going to tell me, are you?"

"Sure I am. Just as soon as you give up. Isn't that what you did?"

Cissy was startled. It *was* what she had done, but it hadn't been an intentional tactic. She laughed, respect for his awareness of nuance showing in her eyes. "I give up. I should have known better than to try to con an Irishman."

"I have a brother, Kevin, who's almost two years younger than I. We've always been close, close as twins, people say. He was hurt in an automobile accident three years ago. That's why I know about therapy, and it's why there's a whirlpool."

"Is he all right?"

"Now he is, but it took a long time. I learned a lot."

"Was he the only one hurt?"

"A girl with him was hurt too, but not as seriously. The other car hit more on his side of the car. He took it badly though. He felt responsible."

"Was he?"

"There wasn't any clear-cut responsibility in the sense you mean. No one was speeding. No one was drunk. It was a rainy night with wet leaves on the roadway. Like most accidents, it just happened."

"Is he an engineer too?"

Desmond laughed. "No, he's a programmer for one of those think-tank off-shoots from M.I.T. In fact, I can't think of anyone who'd enjoy your engineer story more than Kev. I'll have to remember to tell him."

"Do you live together?"

"At home in Brookline." He finished the last of the wine, his eyes alight with mischief. "You know of the legendary reluctance of the Irish to marry, don't you?"

"I'm probably not as up on sociology as I should be."

"How tactfully you put it," he said. "Our way is a throwback to old-country tradition. In Ireland men don't marry until they're in their thirties, even forties. They live at home like dutiful sons."

"It's a tradition being adopted all over the country then. Kids don't leave home the way they used to. Lots of my friends moved back with their families after college. I could do it."

"But for economic reasons. Ours isn't that. We're just lazy." His expression challenged her to accept that.

"I don't believe you."

"I didn't think you would, but it's the truth."

"You probably don't want to marry. That wouldn't

57

surprise me. After all, I don't want to, so why should you?"

"Now, that surprises me. Why don't you want to get married?"

Cissy made a face. "I'm supposed to, aren't I? I guess that's just the trouble then. I can't see burying myself in some man's shadow, picking up after him, and worshiping him for every crumb he throws my way."

"What kind of crumbs?" Desmond pounced. "Crumbs of affection? Or money?"

"Either, I guess. I want to be my own person."

"And you don't think you could be yourself in a marriage?"

"No, I don't. Just look around. How many women can you point to who are both independent and married? It's a contradiction in terms. You can be one or the other, but not both."

"What about my mother?"

"What about her?"

"You don't think she's both?"

"Desmond, I hardly know your mother. I couldn't say. I know *my* mother, though, and my brother Fletcher's wife, Iris. Neither of them can even call their shadows their own."

"Is that what they say, or what you think?"

"It's what I know from observation. You're just not up on the sociology of WASP families if you think we talk about such things."

"Do they want you to marry?"

She sighed. "Of course they do. People in traps hate to see others roaming around free."

"Are you free? Are you happy?"

"Mostly. Nothing is perfect; but, yes, I'm free and

58

happy. I'll be happier when I can walk around and get back to running, of course."

"Speaking of walking around," Desmond said, giving a look at his watch, "can you wait till after the show for dessert?"

"I don't eat dessert very much."

"You have to make an exception tonight if you like cheesecake. Mom left some of hers in the refrigerator for us. We can have it when we get home."

On the way back they reviewed the show and laughingly counted up the number of times they had seen it, nine times between them. The cheesecake was as good as Desmond's anticipation had led her to expect, especially served in the comfortable living room of his parents' home, filled with chintz and wicker and plants.

"Your mother is a wonderful cook," Cissy said when every delicious crumb was gone.

"Another reason I haven't left home," Desmond answered, but with an expression she couldn't fathom, as if he were laughing at a joke he wouldn't share.

"Don't your parents spend the summer here?"

"They go back in the fall, a little more reluctantly each year. But only one more time now."

"Then what will you do? Buy the house from them?"

"Good heavens, no. It's an ark. It'll probably be made into a condo. Families don't want houses like that anymore."

"Even this house is big," Cissy offered. "It must be murder to heat when the wind is coming off the ocean."

"This winter they're having a lot of work done to tighten it up. Mom insists on a big place, so we can all bring our friends here, and of course she hopes for a lot of grandchildren."

"Moira's will be the first? That's nice. I remember how excited my mother was over Fletcher's sons."

"You sound almost approving."

Cissy shot him a glance. "I'm not against families. Just because I don't want it for myself doesn't mean I'm an embittered misanthrope."

"I'm glad to hear it. Now, if you can tell me you sometimes have a soft spot in your heart for unconscious chauvinists, it'll make my evening."

"I don't think it's possible for a man to be an unconscious chauvinist today."

"Don't pick at threads, Cissy."

"When do you expect your parents and Gwen home?"

Desmond laughed out loud at the question. When she sat up straighter, affronted, he moved closer on the couch. "Don't count on them to save you from what you started on the beach. You get only one reprieve like that."

"*I* started? I didn't start anything," she protested.

"You were giving me instructions on the way you like to be kissed, as I remember."

"That's not what I remember, and you didn't answer my question."

"Gwen is staying with friends, and my parents will be out for hours yet. This is a special bash at the golf club, the first party of the season, so Mom will have to hear about everything she's missed since Labor Day," he answered. "Does that satisfy your curiosity?"

His words had the ring of truth, so they struck an apprehensive chord in Cissy, who had needed the reprieve Desmond facetiously recalled in order to break free from his arms on the beach. In fact, she remembered belatedly, she hadn't been the one to break free at all. Desmond had all but peeled her away from him, only to

60

have to support her until she could stand. She wasn't proud of the memory.

She squared herself to him on the couch by hitching back, stopping only when she reached the corner. "Desmond, I know what you must think of me," she began. She got no further.

"What would I think of you?"

"I'd rather not say. But I'm just not like that."

"Are you trying to tell me you're ashamed of responding to a kiss?"

He made it sound so trivial. "It wasn't just 'a kiss,'" she quoted, imitating his tone. "It was the *way* you kissed me."

He hooked his forefinger under her chin, smiling and moving closer and closer. "More complaints, Cissy?"

"That's not what I meant. . . ." But he wasn't listening; he was kissing her. His lips slid softly over hers, sweet as a sigh. The side of his finger held her chin steady, but then it moved along her jaw, tracing the delicate bone to her ear and back to the point again.

When he withdrew his mouth, his thumb rubbed over her lower lip while he watched the teasing motion and her reaction. "Your mouth is so kissable. I've been waiting to do this all evening."

"Desmond, please."

His thumb tugged on her lower lip, gently prying it down just enough so he could run the end of his thumb along her lower teeth. It was a small, unexpected gesture that released in Cissy a surge of warmth she was unprepared to feel. Her lips trembled and she stared, her eyes rounding in alarm, first at Desmond's dark eyes, then at his mouth. Without intending to, she was willing him to kiss her again, if only to stop him from tantalizing her

61

like this. She had survived other kisses, but she wasn't sure she could survive his tender touching.

"You have such pretty little teeth. Sharp." His voice was low and lazy, like the buzz of a honey-laden bee. "When do you bite, hmm? You did tell me you bite."

Cissy closed her eyes, wanting to slap his hand away and at the same time wanting him never to stop. She roused herself to sit straighter, to stop leaning toward him, and took a deep breath. "I didn't mean it that way. You're twisting my words."

Her protest, faint as it was, died with the touch of his lips to hers again. His thumb still hooked over her chin to open her mouth enough to admit the tip of his tongue. He didn't trespass far, just teased the inside of her lower lip and the row of teeth, but Cissy felt she was drowning in delight. His big hand, unbearably warm, flattened on her back to press her close, then moved to cup her bare shoulder, wrapping her securely in his embrace.

The tender, even tentative nature of his kiss changed so gradually Cissy couldn't have marked the moment his exploration began to lay siege to her defenses. The hand at her neck worked into her hair to pull her head back.

"You're so sweet, so soft," he said into her neck. His mouth was hot, blazing a line of kisses down over her collarbone. When she felt him burrowing under the taffeta stretched tightly over her breasts, she realized he had untied the straps of the dress without her even knowing it. He lifted his head to look at her, and she tried to stir. She pressed her hands against his chest to push him away, but he groaned, "Oh, yes, Cissy."

Yes? She sat up. What did he mean, yes?

He let go of her and yanked at his tie. She snatched back her hands, but when the tie was gone he recaptured them, putting them on his chest as he shrugged out of the suit jacket. The heat of his body came through the soft shirting, making her fingers linger.

"I have something of yours, but you have to reclaim it."

Her sixpence.

He unbuttoned the stiff collar button, then brought her hands to the next one. She'd never had so much trouble undoing a button in her life. His eyes were like sources of heat, warming her face as he took in every quiver of her mouth and every responsive blush of color to her cheeks.

"When you blush, your freckles show up more," he teased. "How many do you have?"

"I don't know. Too many." She had done two buttons and was going to stop when he ordered, "More." She kept going, but with increased reluctance.

"Someday I'll count your freckles. Do they fade in winter?"

She knew Desmond was talking to her to keep her from bolting. Part of her wanted to leave, but she knew he wouldn't let her go, nor did she want him to. She was considerably past the length of the chain, so, hesitantly, she retraced her way up the button placket to the coin. It was nestled in the springy mat of his dark chest hair.

After a moment of indecision, Cissy reached her hands to the chain at his neck to lift it away over his head, but he put his hands over hers and brought them to rest against the deep V bared at the opening of his shirt. "Is that so hard? To touch me?" His voice seemed to be coming from under her own skin, so undermining to her resistance was the deep, soft sound. The warmth under her fingers drew her closer. When he held her shoulders to kiss her again she didn't try to pull away, but curled into his arms, even allowing him to lift her onto his lap.

She felt so safe and warm, even with his hand on her

knee, she was content to go on kissing him forever. Her hands were at the back of his head, woven into his thick hair, the sixpence forgotten as she held his head to her mouth. But he lifted his head away slowly, ending the kiss in spite of the way she tried to pull him back. She opened her eyes reluctantly and cried out softly at the dark passion she saw in his eyes. In one fluid motion that demonstrated his impressive strength, Desmond got up, lifting Cissy in his arms, and carried her to the stairs.

Belatedly, an alarm sounded in Cissy's brain and she began to struggle. "Desmond, put me down!"

His grip tightened to secure her from falling. "Not here. You don't want to climb all these stairs." But at the top he headed for her bedroom. The door to the moonlit room opened to his push and closed with a kick so he could put her gently onto the bed. She struggled up to face him, trying to turn to get her feet over the side of the bed. His knee blocked her.

"Desmond, please. This isn't what I want."

Desmond wasn't listening. He misunderstood, deliberately, she was sure, her attempts to get to her feet. He took off her sandals and dropped them to the floor, wearing an air of helpfulness. As if her concern had been for the bedspread!

"You even have pretty toes," he said. He held one foot and rubbed his thumb over the tops of her toes. *Now it's my toes,* she thought wildly. She pulled her feet back, but then his hand settled again on her knee just under the dress. "Does your knee hurt?"

"No." Her voice was sharp. "Desmond, you're not listening to me."

"Of course I am. You said your knee doesn't hurt. That's good." He was caressing her injured knee, making soothing circles with his fingers around the side of her leg.

When she opened her mouth to protest, he covered it with his and leaned against her to topple her slowly back onto the bed. His tongue made a thorough, sweeping search of her mouth that left her feeling bereft when it finally withdrew. His long fingers were at the back of her knee, tracing the crease as if it were the most erotic part of her, and, judging by her response, it was. Lassitude had taken over her body, making it unwilling to obey or even hear the urgent commands of her mind. With her blood thick as honey in her veins, it was no wonder she didn't resist when he lifted her again to a sitting position. Up, down, what difference did it make?

She looped her arms around his shoulders, content to rest her face against his bare chest and listen to the beat of his heart. His hands skimmed her back, then paused at her waist just as he dipped his head to kiss her again. But his lips only teased her with distracting little forays to her neck and ear.

"Do you have any idea how sexy the sound this dress makes really is?" He nipped her earlobe. "Every time you move, it rustles."

It was rustling now. She nodded, almost giggling.

"Have you forgotten your sixpence?"

She had.

"Why don't you take it back?"

Since her hands were already on his neck, it was easy to lift away the chain and place it over her own head. Before the loop of gold fell into place, Desmond parted the back of her dress so the top fell away to reveal the pale perfection of her breasts. She shouldn't have been as surprised as she was to find herself suddenly subject to the intensity of Desmond's dark-eyed scrutiny. The coin settled between her breasts as she reached instinctively for the top of her dress. His hands caught and held hers at her waist.

"Cissy, please. You're so lovely. Let me look at you."

Moonlight from the two large windows highlighted one side of his face as it fell, direct as a spotlight, on her bare skin. His eyes were shadowed, but she felt their burning impact. He released her hands to reach a steadying hand behind her. With the other he traced the golden line from her neck to the nestled sixpence, fingering it as if it were a part of her.

Cissy's hands tangled in his opened shirt as she reached for him. "Desmond, I . . ."

"Shh." He drew her to his chest, absorbing her rippling response to his heat against her sensitive breasts by wrapping her in his arms.

For a moment she surrendered to the magic, not even breathing, every sense heightened almost to the point of pain. When she felt him pull back slightly, bending to search for her mouth, she gathered her scattered defenses and pushed free. "No, Desmond, please, don't." Her voice was shaky, more plea than statement. "I couldn't live through another kiss."

"What about me?" he croaked. "God, Cissy, I ache for you."

What could she say? She ached, too, but it was too soon. She pulled up her dress and reached behind her back to redo the ties. The process arched her back in unintended provocation, and he reached for her. His hands covered her breasts against the dress, searing through the cloth as if it weren't there.

"I'm not going to make the mistake of calling you a tease again," he said unevenly, "but the word comes to mind."

She had finished, but he didn't let go. "You could have helped me."

He laughed raggedly. "No way. I've done all I'm doing against my best interests tonight." His thumbs worried her nipples, making her close her eyes.

"Don't make it harder, Desmond. I just can't."

"Yet," he finished for her. His hands went to her shoulders and he kissed her mouth, hard, before he drew back. "I hope you have as much trouble getting to sleep tonight as I'm going to have." Then he was gone.

CHAPTER FIVE

Two dresses hung on the closet door awaiting Cissy's decision. Both were new, both reflected Cissy's recent, more feminine image. Her birthday money was gone now, and she would have to scrimp this month to pay for it all, but looking at her purchases again, she decided having the dresses was compensation enough for poverty. She hadn't been able to choose between them in the store and she still couldn't.

Since she was going to an outdoor Pops concert with Desmond, she thought perhaps the floral print would be best. She could wear comfortable sandals with that. There was bound to be a lot of walking in getting from wherever they would park to the site of the Esplanade on the Charles River.

Walking was again possible, even almost enjoyable. She was pleased by her recovery, even if Lucky still wasn't. The exercises Desmond suggested helped almost as much as his encouragement. She still kept the crutches against the bathroom door, available once in a while when she was tired or when she had sat long enough for the knee to have stiffened, but she wouldn't use them tonight.

She hung the green dress in her closet for another time,

reasonably confident now that there would be another time with Desmond. The night he had left her bedroom on the cape she had been almost certain she'd never see him again once he delivered her to her apartment the next day. Now she knew differently, although she still didn't know quite what to make of him. He hadn't pressed her since that night, but if they continued to spend time together, they would have to find a way to deal with the potent attraction between them. Desmond had evidently backed off to give her time to get to know him, but then what?

Desmond was too charming, too perfect, to be anything but irresistible. And she had to resist him. There were already too many men in her life telling her what to do, for one thing. She had a coach, a boss, a father, and a brother. She didn't have room for him, but he wouldn't be able to understand her reluctance. He would think she was holding out for marriage in spite of what she said. With his family background he'd never believe she really didn't want to marry. This injury-ridden time was just an interlude in her life. Her future was running. She wouldn't let herself get sidetracked by falling in love. Desmond was the marrying kind. She was not. It was that simple and that complex.

What she didn't know was how to make a man like Desmond understand her feelings. She wasn't afraid of sex, but she was terrified of sex with Desmond. She would fall in love with him. Then where would she be with her career and all her plans? She could perhaps handle it if he were just some shallow individual with shoulders. But Desmond was so much more than shoulders and savvy. Him she couldn't handle. She didn't dare even try.

"Saved by the bell," she said aloud when the phone

69

called her from her pointless ruminations. But she felt less saved when she understood her mother's message. Fletcher's wife, Iris, had taken their two small boys back home to Mother in Connecticut, saying she wanted a divorce. Fletcher had just come to tell the story and her mother wanted her there.

In a daze Cissy phoned Desmond to break their date. His questions cut to the heart of Cissy's involvement, but his conclusion differed from hers.

"I'll pick you up in Lexington and take you home to change. We can buy our food in your neighborhood and go to the concert anyway."

"But I'll have my car."

"I'll drive you to get it back tomorrow."

"But . . ."

"Don't fuss, Cissy. She didn't leave the children behind, so you won't be needed to care for them. There's only so much you can do to help your parents. Give me the directions to the house—no, just the address. I'll find it."

"Desmond . . ."

"The address."

She gave it resentfully, satisfying herself by slamming down the receiver hard enough to jar the bell. Men! No wonder Iris left Fletcher. They were all alike. What had ever possessed her to think Desmond was different?

She was still fuming when she pulled her car into the circular drive behind her family's cars. At the head stood Joseph F. Barlow's silver Continental. Brother Fletcher Joseph drove the next in line, a gray Buick. Mother Margaret's cream-colored Chrysler rested safely in the garage, thereby allowing Cissy's ancient yellow Volvo, like a caboose, to strike the single note of comic relief.

What fun a sociologist would have analyzing her

family's relationships, she thought. Using no evidence that couldn't be seen from the street, her mythical expert would be able to read them like a book. The gracious Colonial-style house, well set back from the shaded street, obviously aspired to combine making a statement about business success with family comfort. Status was more the concern of the front yard than the back, where Cissy noticed that the play area, long ago hers, showed recent use. She shut the back gate on her way to the kitchen door, thinking how her mother must find Joey's abandoned plastic wheelbarrow a poignant reminder that he and his brother might not play there much in the future.

Her mother and Fletcher were drinking coffee at the large round oak table in the kitchen, and although she protested their rising, both got to their feet automatically, Fletcher to greet a woman, Margaret to fetch another cup and saucer.

"Glad to see you walking on your own again. How's the knee?"

"Okay. How are you?" She searched his face for evidence of anguish as they sat down. Like her father, whom he resembled, Fletcher's emotions were under tight control. He was as fair as Cissy was, with only a betraying floridity to give away his agitation. And his thin lips straightened to a grim line across his lower face, she noted, completing her survey.

"I'm okay. Mad as hell, but I guess you've already figured that out."

She looked away to accept her coffee. "Where's Dad?" she asked her mother.

"Watching the game." It being summer, the game was baseball, preferably the Red Sox, but in desperation to avoid unpleasantness he would watch anything that flickered on television.

Into the strained silence Cissy asked, "Has anyone talked to Iris?"

"Anyone" was certainly meant to be Fletcher, but Margaret spoke up. "I would have called her, but Fletcher said not to."

"Have you called?"

"No, and I don't intend to."

Cissy stared at him.

His face reddened. "Damn it! I should have known better than to expect any sympathy from you. You probably put her up to the whole thing."

"You know that's not true. I haven't even spoken to her on the phone since before the cape race. I'm hardly her confidante. Maybe I should have tried to be closer, but she never seemed to need or want anyone but you and the boys." Her phrasing made her start, her eyes widening in alarm at the unspoken question she couldn't keep from her mind.

Fletcher laughed bitterly. "No, Cissy, there isn't anyone else for either of us. And I didn't beat her or get drunk." His expression said both activities looked increasingly attractive to him. "The note said I don't respect her enough. I don't value her as a person." The words were venomous.

"And you still haven't tried to contact her? Since Tuesday?"

"I figured it was just a ploy to get me to grovel."

"But Fletcher . . ."

"I thought she'd cool down and come back, at least by today."

He'd only told his parents this afternoon, she knew. "Since that didn't happen, are you going to call now?"

"I don't know."

Cissy opened her mouth, then shut it firmly. She looked from her tight-lipped brother to her mother. Margaret looked weepy and embarrassed, her eyes darting from one to the other of her children. "How are you, Mom? How's Dad?" Cissy asked finally.

Typically placing herself last, she answered, "Dad's taking it pretty hard, but I'm okay." With an imploring look to Cissy, she added, "Did you have lunch? I couldn't get Fletcher to eat anything."

He got to his feet in disgust. "You think everything can be cured by food. I'm going to watch the game."

The last was flung at Cissy, who was ready to explode with anger. Margaret patted her hand with timid but insistent little strokes meant to be soothing. "Now, don't get upset. He doesn't mean half of what he says. He's just got to blow off some steam. It's an awful blow for a man to have to tell anyone his wife has left him, even if it is only for a while."

"What makes you so sure it's not permanent? Did she say something to you? It'll *be* permanent if he doesn't wise up. No one like Iris runs off without a lot of pent-up anger behind it."

"Well, no, of course not—to both things." She laughed a little, as if pleased to have sorted out Cissy's tirade. "I don't know, dear. I thought I understood Iris. I thought she was as happy as I was years ago with my little family."

"She probably was, Mom. It's just that things have changed a lot since then. Women want more respect, more sensitivity, from their husbands. And you have to admit, Fletcher isn't exactly the 'new man.' "

"Whatever that is," Margaret murmured. "I guess I

didn't do very well preparing him for marriage. I waited on him too much."

"He'd need a harem to replace all you did for him," Cissy said stoutly, then she exploded in laughter at the shocked look on her mother's face. "Oh, Mom, you really are priceless!"

"I'm glad you can find something to laugh about," Fletcher said, having lost interest almost immediately in the ballgame. He looked even grimmer than before, disapproval of their frivolity stamped on every feature.

"Of course we can, brother dear. We're women, and you know how women are, don't you?" Cissy gave him a syrupy smile and departed from the room, knowing her mother would soothe his ruffled feathers. She went to the den and, after planting a kiss on her father's balding head, joined him on the couch. Men weren't supposed to follow their fathers' pattern of hair loss, but Fletcher would someday be just as bald as his father, she thought irrelevantly.

"How're you doing, Gimpy?" he asked gruffly.

"No more Gimpy." In a flash of annoyance she realized he hadn't taken his eyes from the set to look at her. "Really, Dad, is the game so great?"

"It stinks."

"Honestly!"

"Just wait till this guy is out."

Cissy sat in rigid silence until he leaned forward and lowered the sound. "It's a wonder Mom didn't leave years ago."

"She's made of sterner stuff than you young women."

"No. We're made of sterner stuff. That's why we're trying to shape you men up."

"She knows I'm too old to change. Thank God.

74

Women today say they want men who cry!" He made it sound revolting.

"Why not? It's an expression of human emotion."

He snorted in derision. "Can you run yet?"

"No, but I can walk, and I'm pretty happy about that."

"Is Lucky?"

"You know Lucky. He wouldn't appreciate me walking on water."

"Do you work out?"

"Therapy and lots of weights. I'm going to be the strongest fat lady in the world."

"You are getting plumper. Lucky might not approve, but he's the only man who wouldn't."

"How are you doing?"

"She's a fool!" he exploded. His naturally florid face deepened to a dangerous-looking red.

Cissy tried to smile. "Dad, that's not an answer to my question."

"Of course it is."

She tried again, saying gently, "It's their problem, Dad. Whatever happens, it's no reflection on you."

"Haven't you learned better than that even at that Mickey Mouse bank where you work?" First Fiduciary had once refused financing to expand Barlow Security Systems, earning Joseph Barlow's eternal enmity.

"Divorce is common now, Dad. If a divorce could bring down a business, there would only be about five going concerns in the country."

"Tell that to our board of directors."

"You don't have to tell them anything. Fletcher will do his job. His personal life is no one's business."

"Hmph." The game had already reclaimed his attention, so after a few minutes Cissy returned to the kitchen, offering a shrug to her mother's questioning gaze.

Fletcher got up immediately, asking, "Want to shoot a little pool?"

"Sure." Margaret beamed approval of them as they went to the recreation room at the back of the garage. Of their teenage paraphernalia, all that remained to stem the rising tide of grandchildren's toys was the bumper pool table and a wall display of sports trophies. Their play was desultory, merely an excuse for being alone, but when Fletcher still didn't broach the subject, Cissy did. "What are you going to do?"

"I really don't know. I'm so angry I'm not thinking straight."

"Why angry? Why not hurt or scared?"

"Because she knew this was a bad time for me. I have that presentation for Laird Chemical next week, and she purposely picked now to pull her little stunt."

"Did you ever think that maybe it isn't a little stunt, and maybe she didn't choose her timing so diabolically? After all, Fletcher, unless you're a lot different from Dad —which I very much doubt—there's never anything but a bad time for you. You always have something special going on. Maybe she just reached her limit and couldn't help herself."

He pretended to give his shot grave consideration.

"Do you love her? Do you want your family?"

"Of course I want my family!" The shot was a disaster.

"Then why don't you go after her? If you throw over the Laird deal for her, she'll be impressed. Ask her parents to take the kids while you and Iris go somewhere and make up."

Fletcher straightened up to look at her, revealing him-

76

self momentarily before he hid the pain in his eyes by bending to the table again.

"You have to do it, you know. The ball is in your court."

He threw down the cue and glared at her. "I don't know what to say."

"Then listen. That's the best thing to do anyway. Find out what she feels and what she wants—without getting angry—then tell her what you feel and want. See how you can each get something out of the future situation. She doesn't want to bring up two little boys alone. You can't doubt that she loves you."

Fletcher ran his hand through his thinning hair in a gesture Iris probably loved. "What makes you so damned smart anyway? You're not even married." He stepped back to give her room to set up her shot.

"I have the wisdom of the eternal female in my bones. That's also why I'm not married."

"Also nobody's asked you," he countered.

"Oh, no? John Brady asked me in fifth grade."

"Brady? Isn't he the one who's doing time at Walpole?"

Cissy turned on him, raising her cue stick menacingly, only to have it taken from behind her. She whirled in surprise. "Desmond, you sneak! How did you get in here?"

"I followed your mother's directions." He offered his hand to her brother. "You must be Fletcher. Desmond McGinnis. I try to keep weapons like this away from your sister."

Cissy noted the approval in Fletcher's assessing glance and covered her pleasure by accusing: "You're early."

Fletcher put down his cue. "That's just as well. It seems I have a trip to take, so you can take over for me here. She's not very good at this, but she has her uses." His smile thanked her as he backed away. "Nice to meet you, Desmond."

When she turned back to Desmond he was studying the trophies. "Fletcher played football," he commented.

"He did everything. For years I wanted to be him—not just be like him, but *be* him. I was miserable until I discovered I could run. It was bad enough being a girl, but when I didn't have the hand-eye coordination for tennis, or even softball or basketball, I wanted to die. Then I fell in love with my feet and decided to live."

"When was that?"

"I was sixteen. I had managed to swim, but my true destiny didn't show up until a gym teacher found out I was fleet."

"I'm glad you decided to live. Do you want to play?" He gestured to the table.

"It was just a way to get away from Mom and Dad to talk."

"Can you leave?"

"Sure. Did you meet Dad?"

He hadn't, but by the time Cissy had given him the tour of her backyard the game had ended, freeing Joseph for social amenities. His version of conversation wasn't subtle, but Desmond handled the grilling with tact and aplomb, neither taking offense nor letting himself be walked over. Before they could leave, Margaret made them promise to stop for dinner when they picked up Cissy's car the next day.

"I knew it was a mistake to have you come here," Cissy grumbled when she was inside his vintage Volkswagen. "Tomorrow night when I walk into the apartment my phone will be ringing."

He laughed. "Your mother."

"Would your mother do that?"

"Don't you think she already has?"

"But it's embarrassing. They act as if they're desperate to marry me off, regardless of what I say."

"It's natural. They want you to be happy."

"Sure. See how happy Fletcher is."

"How did that go?"

"He's a jerk."

"Do I note a general condemnation of my sex in that remark?"

"You do. But Iris is a jerk too. They deserve each other."

"That's comforting. Now, is there somewhere around here we can get the food for our picnic, or shall we go nearer your place?"

"We can get great subs on my street, and anyway I want to change."

"No subs. This is going to be elegant."

"In that case, I definitely have to change."

They shopped in Harvard Square to fill Desmond's hamper with carefully selected cheeses, coldcuts, hearty bread, and loganberry tarts until Cissy protested she wouldn't have time to change from her cut-off jeans.

"I can help," Desmond volunteered. "I'm very good with zippers."

"You can help by staying in the car. Besides, the dress doesn't have a zipper," she lied.

"I'm taking notes." He put the basket into the back-seat. Before he started the car he kissed her nose and let one hand glide up the length of her leg. "It's a shame to cover up those legs though. I don't suppose it's a mini?"

She shook her head. Trying to change the subject, she asked, "How come you're not on the cape? Aren't your parents there?"

"They are, but you're not, and right now I'm pursuing you. Next weekend we can go to the cape. We have a standing invitation."

Cissy looked blindly forward at the car parked ahead of them. She could feel him watching her intently. It was almost a relief when he turned her face to his.

"Tonight we're going to talk, Mary Elizabeth Rose." It was a vow he sealed with a firm kiss before he turned the key. "You told me all your names, but not why so many."

Answering distracted her from considering the lump of unease forming under her breastbone. "Mom had three aunts she loved. She knew I was going to be her last child, so she dumped all the honor on me." His unspoken question hovered, so she added, "She had cesareans and two was all her doctor allowed."

As if he understood he'd disconcerted her, Desmond kept a stream of soothing chatter flowing the rest of the way to her apartment. While she changed, he occupied himself in the tiny kitchen, repacking their food and selecting utensils to suit their needs, but still Cissy dressed nervously.

The dress no longer pleased her. It was as form-fitting as the taffeta and, under the tiny jacket, as bare-shouldered too. Doing up the back zipper, she tried to assure herself that the dress wasn't seductive, but still Desmond gave her an appreciative whistle before he sent her back for a blanket they could use on the grass.

Others carried beach chairs, even hibachis, to the concert, making the air as redolent with scent as with music. Two blankets away a flutist played along on his own instrument, winning applause from all who could hear him for the expert way he followed John Williams's baton. Cissy leaned back against Desmond and let the music waft over her. She reveled in the weight of his arm casually cast over her shoulder and filed away in her mind the way the breeze ruffled his dark hair even as it blew the sound in volleys that distorted the perfect music. She drank the wine slowly, careful not to lose the edge of perceptiveness that made such complete awareness possible.

In the back of her mind she heard the words, unspoken so far, Desmond would use to persuade her into lovemaking. Common sense and even her own body bargained on his side, leaving her nothing but her own intense need to remain her own person. The weeks of injury-induced physical inactivity had forced her into unaccustomed introspection, but from it she had wrung a new sense of herself and of her purpose in life. There was no room for Desmond in that life. She would only fall in love with him. Then where would she be? She knew. She'd be hurt in ways that would never heal.

In spite of everything she could do to preserve each moment, to slow down the flight of time, inevitably the concert ended, the applause faded, and the crowd dispersed. Cissy did little to help, but finally she had to follow Desmond and carry the blanket he thrust into her reluctant arms. He reached the car first and turned to look back at her as he put the picnic hamper into the backseat.

"You look like Marie Antoinette going to the guillotine." He laughed. She put the blanket into his arms and sat in the front without comment. She knew he was looking at her when he failed to start the car as soon as he got in, but she couldn't meet his eyes. She waited like a stone for him to drive, and finally he did, but not before she heard the small sigh of exasperation that accompanied the action.

Like an automaton she unpacked the leftover food and

washed the few dishes, glasses, and flatware pieces they had used, all under Desmond's watchful eye. She cleaned the sink and shut every cupboard door.

"Are you sure your shelves don't need new lining papers? Maybe you should defrost the freezer while you're here?"

Cissy stiffened, then slowly let her shoulders relax. "It's a frost-free model," she said flippantly. He didn't laugh or even smile as he weighed her on some scale she couldn't imagine. When the intensity of his scrutiny became intolerable, she turned toward the small living room, but before she could make it through the doorway he lifted her into his arms. In the living room he seemed to consider the couch for a second, but the narrow bed in her bedroom was his inevitable destination. She didn't struggle or protest, trying for total passivity even as he loomed above her at the side of the bed.

When he bent to kiss her she turned her head quickly. "I thought you said we were going to talk," she accused him.

He sat back up, one hand beside her waist, the other resting on his thigh. "Ever since I said that you've been looking like a lost puppy. I thought perhaps we should get reacquainted first." He lifted his hand from his leg to smooth back her hair and cup her cheek.

The tenderness of the gesture eroded her control. "We don't really know each other, so reacquaintance isn't possible."

His laugh was short. "So prickly." The only light came from the living room behind him, so she couldn't see his face clearly. "I've met your family and been to your house. You've done the same. There's a physical attraction between us that you feel as strongly as I do. I'd call that acquaintance after three weeks." His thumb stroked her chin and lips. "So talk," he urged. "Tell me what I need to know to be well acquainted with you."

The words struck her dumb. She closed her eyes, her body so rigid only the part of her face he touched seemed alive. She held her breath as he leaned forward.

"Then let's try it my way instead," he said softly against her lips.

His kiss was what she wanted, and under the warm pressure of his mouth she relaxed enough to breathe superficially again. The kiss was comforting and undemanding. It didn't change even when he stretched himself out beside her and took her into his arms. She felt so safe with him. Her mind knew it was an illusion, but her body responded to the sheltering support of his arms and the consoling warmth of his body. In spite of herself his warmth began to melt her rigidity and she nestled deeper into his embrace. His mouth moved coaxingly on her stiff lips, finally sliding to her ear.

"Open to me, sweetheart. Let me really kiss you." The words blazed to life in her mind, making her helpless to resist the blossoming ache of desire within her. His mouth didn't return to hers until it had traveled all over her face and lingered tantalizingly just beside her now eager mouth. Even then he held back, only darting his tongue to flick against the roof of her mouth. She held his head with both hands, but still he didn't take the liberties she offered until she touched his tongue with hers. His reaction was a breathtaking plunge into passionate possession. His tongue filled her with stroking heat. He explored and tasted all she gave, retreating only to incite her into reciprocation.

She was so busy discovering the wonder of his mouth she didn't notice that he'd removed her jacket until it was gone. He put her hand over his heart and held it there.

"Feel what you do to me. I think I'm having a heart attack."

"I know how to do CPR," she whispered.

"Just your kiss would revive a dead man, sweetheart." He took her mouth again as he covered one breast with his hand. The crisp cotton of the dress seemed to melt away under his covering heat and she moved against him. It felt so good for him to touch her, she ignored the downward slide of her zipper. His thumb rubbed over her tight nipple, teasing it and distracting her from protesting when he pushed the wide strap down over her shoulder, loosening the unzipped dress. Through it all, his mouth never left hers, never relinquished control of her senses. When he pushed the top of her dress down, baring her breast to nestle in his palm, Cissy stiffened briefly in protest, but soon melted under the onslaught of new sensations.

Though she tried to keep him close, he pulled away to look at her. She couldn't open her eyes, but she knew when his eyes left her face because he took his hand from her breast. She fought the deep feeling of desire that suddenly swelled inside her. She dragged her eyes open just in time to see Desmond bend to seek her breast. Her hands gripped his head and pulled his face up to hers.

"Desmond, please, don't." She didn't try to hide the desperation in her eyes as he froze watchfully, his face inches from hers.

"You don't want me to love you? Is that what you're saying?"

His expression frightened her. It was grim and hard. She swallowed back a choking laugh and pushed back from him to fix her dress. "Don't confuse the issue. We're not talking about love, just *making* love."

He sat back, unmoved. "And you don't want me making love to you."

"It's too soon." It was too fragile a vessel to hold all her defenses and she knew it, but she launched it anyway, knowing it was all she had.

"You have a timetable all worked out then?"

"Don't be spiteful. This is hard for me too." His face didn't soften, so she pressed on. "You were the one who wanted to talk."

"So I did." He relented then and gave her a half-hearted grin. "I was hoping we could skip it though. I'm trying to be patient, but my patience only goes so far. I'm going to love you sooner or later, you know, so this arbitrary schedule of yours makes no sense to me."

"You want too much from me. I just can't handle that."

"It will be good, sweetheart. Don't you know that yet?"

"No, I really don't," she lied, then, more truthfully, went on. "I'm a little low on trust. I don't even trust myself, much less you."

"What about the way we feel?"

"Physical attraction isn't reliable. I've been to that show." Cissy tried to read his reaction to that bald statement. If he was surprised, he didn't show it. "Desmond, you're a special man. I'm just not what you want."

He laughed, shaking his head ruefully. "I've been turned down before, you know, but never because I was too special. You are something else, Mary Elizabeth Rose." He looked over at the empty twin bed across the room. "I don't suppose you'd let me spend the night there, would you?"

She shook her head, relief making her almost giddy. "Not even on the couch."

"Will your roommate be back?"

Cissy considered lying, then shook her head.

"Then I'll come back in the morning." He leaned forward to kiss her nose lightly. She started to offer her lips, then thought better of it as he got up to leave.

When he was at the door she couldn't keep from calling out to him. He turned and she said simply, "Thank you."

The look he gave her was more indulgent than she had any right to expect. "Stow it, Cissy."

CHAPTER SIX

It took Cissy a long time to get to sleep after Desmond left. She had a lot of recriminations to get through before she was calm enough to think. And while he had accepted her dictum gracefully—more gracefully than she would have in his place—she knew she'd won only a brief period of time before they would either discuss it all again or he would sweep aside her paltry objections. She knew the only solution for her would be to stop seeing him altogether. But how could she do that, when already she doted on his smile and on that uniquely humorous sensuality of his that made her feel womanly for the first time in her life?

She paced the room, exchanged the dress for a stretched-out T-shirt, did some sit-ups, then stalked to the shower in self-disgust. She couldn't begin to think why Desmond was attracted to her. She wasn't brilliant or witty or beautiful. She could run fast, that was all. He was the kind of man every other woman was looking for, a sexy, smart man who wouldn't shy away from commitment. Someday she might even want a man like that too. But not now. It was too soon. She wasn't ready for the suburbs and her 2.5 children. She blasted herself with a final rinse of cold water and dashed for a towel. The T-shirt she'd taken off lay soaked on the floor, the bikinis, too, so she found fresh panties and a faded tank top to wear to bed.

The pillow still carried the slight scent of Desmond's spicy aftershave. She groaned aloud as that small reminder of him flooded her senses. She turned the pillow over angrily, then stared at the shadowed ceiling. After several tense minutes she rolled onto her stomach and turned the pillow again so she could bury her face there. Strangely soothed, she finally fell asleep.

Desmond knew it was too early to go to Cissy's apartment, but he'd waked with the birds, taken his run, and showered. He had the key Cissy had forgotten to take back burning a hole in his palm. He had no right to use it, but he knew he would. Unless she'd thrown what looked like a dozen locks bristling on the inside of the door.

He knocked, softly, and tried the knob. After another token knock he fit the key into the lock and turned it. The door opened, proving she had done nothing to secure the apartment after he'd left. Pleased for his own sake, he couldn't help his irrational concern that she'd carelessly left herself vulnerable to someone else. He laughed soundlessly as he considered her response to a lecture from him on security.

Everything was just as he had left it, even the half-open bedroom door. He paused at the threshold long enough to determine that Cissy slept soundly and was still alone. In the kitchen he searched the cabinets for the can of coffee he'd noticed yesterday. Freshly perked coffee would be his apology for coming in this way.

He put the coffee, hers whitened the way she liked it

with that powdered cream, beside the bed and looked at the back of her tousled hair and outflung arm. He didn't miss the twisted sheet and slender bare foot and ankle that betrayed the fact that her restlessness through the night had equaled his, and fought down the impulse to take her into his arms. What he wanted to do would have shocked the almost childlike innocence from her forever. He waited until the coffee aroma and his silent watchfulness penetrated her sleep, then sat on the edge of the bed and let her roll right into his arms when she turned over.

"What on earth . . . Desmond?"

He pulled her into a rough approximation of a sitting position and put the cup and saucer into her hands. "Be careful, that's hot." His hands hovered near hers, ready to prevent a serious spill, but he could see she didn't notice that. The spoon rattled and she tightened her grip.

"You left. I know you did. What are you *doing* here?" She started to slip down, remembered the coffee, sat up, then, mindful of the skimpiness of her attire, slid lower. "Take this damn coffee," she demanded crossly. "Go away and let me sleep."

"Drink it. It will make you feel better."

"I don't want to feel better. I want to sleep." She reached to put the cup on the bedside table, twisting beguilingly against the coral jersey. When she was safely back beneath the sheet, her mind began to clear. "How did you get in here?" Her eyes widened as she answered her own question. "I never got back the key." She looked at the coffee on the table. "That was mean. *You're* mean. Where did you ever pick up a trick like that?"

"From my dad. He used to get us going that way on school mornings."

"With coffee?"

"Orange juice. Believe me, you didn't want cold juice in your bed either."

"And I thought he was nice."

"He is nice, just like me. After the first few times it was actually a better way to start the day than being nagged at repeatedly and still missing the school bus." He put the coffee back into her hands. "Drink up. You'll be safer holding that."

She was awake enough to understand, and to blush a bit as well. Desmond held his own cup of black coffee as further back-up, but he couldn't keep his eyes under the same control. He saw her notice and react with a purely feminine smile of satisfaction.

"Don't push it," he warned in a low voice, swallowing the coffee in several rapid throat-tingling gulps. He got up and paced away. She was watching him, her eyes wide, pleading, but for what?

"I'll give you five minutes to get going. If you're not out of bed by then, I'm coming to join you and we'll forget all about breakfast."

"Desmond!" she wailed.

"Five minutes." At the door he looked back in time to see her drop the sheet and kneel to put down the cup. He shut the door on her half-clad form just before her pillow hit the door with a soft thud. He didn't try to move for a long time. He knew she'd get up. Damn.

Cissy was tempted to stay in bed and call Desmond's bluff, taking the easy way out of her frustration. And she was frustrated. He hadn't even kissed her, for Pete's sake! He'd just sat there looking at her as if she were the last lambchop on the platter, making her want to fling herself at him.

She stared at the closed door and slid flat on the bed,

smiling in spite of herself. He might as well be the devil himself as far as she was concerned. Staying out of bed with him wasn't doing much to keep her from falling in love with him.

On that disconcerting thought she finished off the coffee and went to shower away her cobwebs. She dressed in teal blue twill slacks and a matching camisole edged with crocheting before she replaced the pillow on the straightened bed.

She found Desmond staring balefully into her refrigerator. "Do you realize you have no bacon, only two eggs, and no milk? What do you live on?"

"Not bacon and eggs, I assure you." She refilled her coffee cup and leaned against the counter looking at him. He wore tan slacks and a gingham shirt with the sleeves rolled back over his hair-covered forearms. "Bacon has chemicals and eggs are full of cholesterol. There's orange juice and toast."

"Man does not live by bread and juice, nor woman either. No wonder you're a flyweight."

"Is that a category of boxing weight or the insect? I've always wondered."

"Don't change the subject. I'm hungry."

"Would some apple pancakes suit you?"

"You can't make pancakes without milk."

"I have nonfat powdered milk, smartie. It's what I always use."

"Sounds terrible, but I'm desperate. Does it work?"

"Reserve judgment until you try."

"We could go out to eat."

"I have real Vermont maple syrup." When his eyes brightened she handed him an apple and a paring knife as she started the electric griddle heating.

"You're not a vegetarian, are you?" he asked.

"You know I'm not. Remember the scallops? I eat what I like basically, but I do try to eat more carbohydrates than fats and animal proteins. The dry milk is handy. It doesn't go sour and it's healthful."

In spite of his misgivings he liked the pancakes, even without real butter, which she also didn't have. Still, he chided her for using only cinnamon-sugar on hers instead of the pale gold syrup, asking, "Are you dieting?"

"Not really, but I'm not running now, so I can't eat like a stevedore. I don't have much of a taste for sweets anyway. The apple and cinnamon satisfy me."

They did the dishes together and she put them away.

"Are you always this neat?" he asked as she shut the last door and folded the dishcloth over the faucet.

"I guess so." She took in his speculative look. "Why the third degree? Do you think I'm trying to impress you with what a nice little housewife I'll make?"

He grinned. "Of course you are. Deep in your unconscious mind there's a dormant *hausfrau* fighting to get past the liberated career woman you try to—"

She didn't let him finish. "You insufferable . . ." All she could find to throw at him was the dishcloth, which he caught and tossed back into the sink. She wanted to launch herself at him, but she knew where that would lead. Instead, she refolded the dishcloth with hands that trembled slightly.

"Chicken," he taunted.

She laughed. "You're too willing."

He looped his arm over her shoulder and pulled her against him. "So are you, if you want to know."

"I don't." She wanted to kiss him, but the banked fires in his dark eyes were too ready to flare, so she held herself stiffly within the circle of his long arms.

He kissed her cheek and closed her eyes with his lips.

"You're going to have a lot to make up to me for after this morning. Lord, what you do to a jersey! Do you always dress like that for bed?"

"I wear whatever I can get my hands on. I don't have special nightgowns, if that's what you're asking."

He gave a strangled sound and put her, unkissed, at arm's length from him. "I have to be a masochist," he muttered. "Come on. Let's take a walk."

Without a plan, they ended up ambling down Beacon Hill to a kiosk by the Public Garden where they bought two Sunday papers to read under a willow tree by the Mill Pond. Since both wanted the same section of the *Globe* first, they used the fatter *New York Times* as a headrest and shared the sports pages, squabbling good-humoredly about their differing reading speeds. Feeling drowsy and at peace, Cissy gave up her share of the paper and divided her attention between the tourist-laden swan boats and two boys playing Frisbee.

"Have you ever been in love?"

Desmond's question caught her by surprise. "No, not really. I thought I was a few times though." She narrowed her eyes against the sun behind him. His hair looked like dark fire in the bright rays. "How about you?"

"I used to fall in love every other week," he laughed.

"But not anymore?" Waiting for his answer, she held her breath, even though she knew he wouldn't treat the question seriously.

"Not anymore," he agreed. His expression told her he knew he hadn't told her anything. "What's the name of the guy you went out with last?"

"Last?" She had to think. "Hedrick Ames. He works at the bank. Very pinstriped. He's my escort when I have to be proper." She rolled over onto her stomach and propped up on her elbows. "And the name of your last date?"

He laughed. "I've forgotten her name. Moria foisted her off on me. She was on the rebound from some guy Moira doesn't approve of."

"Then Moira lives around here too?"

"In Belmont. She and Neil have their first house."

"You sound envious." Cissy watched his face carefully, expecting instant denial.

"Of course. Their kind of happiness merits envy."

She shook her head, puzzled.

"You don't understand that? Don't you have friends you envy, friends who've found their mate?"

"My high school friends are all getting divorces now. I don't envy anyone."

"You will when you meet Moira. She glows with happiness. She was always lovely—like you," he added absently, "but now that she's pregnant, she's gorgeous."

Cissy laughed incredulously. "I've never seen a gorgeous pregnant woman."

Desmond's smile was complacent. *"You* will be a gorgeous pregnant woman."

She rolled away from him to sit up, totally disconcerted. She began to gather up their papers. "We should be getting back."

Desmond watched, getting to his feet when she was again composed. He took the bundled newspapers from her and draped his arm over her shoulders so she had to walk close to his side. Their return was silent, but after a while the silence grew companionable again, and Cissy felt less assailed by the intensity of his attention. She knew the picture they made together, both from their reflection in store windows and from the occasional envious or understanding second glance from others. They looked like lovers. The picture was so appealing to Cissy, she forgot what she'd told Desmond minutes ago and envied that image of herself. If only it were true.

The air in the apartment seemed stale after being outdoors, so Desmond opened windows while she made more coffee to go with the bagels they had bought.

"You know, of course, Mom will have roast beef and Yorkshire pudding for dinner," she warned Desmond as he reached for a second bagel from the coffee table.

"I think I can handle that. What time do we leave?" He touched his forefinger to the corner of her mouth and carried an overlooked smudge of cream cheese to his lips, licking it away unselfconsciously. The intimacy of the gesture and his naturalness stunned Cissy, making her first stare at him, then turn away in confusion.

Desmond put the bagel back onto the plate and gathered her into his arms. "I shock you, don't I?"

She was embarrassed, so she tried to joke. "Haven't you ever heard of germs?"

"Lovers don't have germs," he said gently.

"We're not lovers."

"We will be. We can be right now. We already are in all but fact." He shot a glance at his watch. "All you have to do is call your mother and tell her to hold the roast beef for an hour. I don't want to rush."

She had to laugh or he'd know how he affected her, how she wanted to do just what he said. She shook her head. She tried, vainly, to imagine herself being bold enough to walk to the phone and delay dinner to allow time for making love. The possibility teased at her mind. She felt his eyes on her face and knew he understood her desire.

He kissed her softly. "It will happen. I'm patient, persistent, and aggressive. It's a winning combination." His hands bracketed her small face. "I can't wait to see your face when you discover how good you can feel."

Cissy sat helplessly, waiting for him to kiss her. She heard the small impatient sound she made without realizing it came from her. His lips finally touched hers and she closed her eyes with a sigh. The sound of the telephone had no reality until Desmond drew back with a laugh. "That's your mother. Dinner is going to be delayed."

He was right, but it wasn't cause for elation.

CHAPTER SEVEN

They found Margaret Barlow on a wooden bench deep in the labyrinth of the hospital's emergency area. It was too big to be called a room, Cissy decided, relieved to see that although her mother's eyes sparkled with unshed tears she hadn't collapsed in hysteria. She embraced Cissy and took Desmond's hand.

"He's being evaluated now." Immediately she answered the unspoken question, waving her hand to the area behind an open fortress of a desk. "They won't admit him until the doctor gets here."

"You mean he hasn't seen a doctor yet?" Cissy asked sharply.

"No, no, dear. Dr. Morse saw him at home. There are doctors checking him now, too, but a Dr. Woodman is going to care for him here and *he's* not here yet."

"They're sure it was a stroke?"

"I don't know. Dr. Morse seemed to think so." Her brows knit together. "It's what his father had," she added softly.

"Why here, Mom?" The bleakness of exposed pipes and abandoned storage carts around them made it hard to feel hopeful. A wailing ambulance siren snarled to a stop somewhere outside, but where they waited no one seemed to notice.

"Dr. Morse said it's the best place. He interned here at Mass General with Dr. Woodman. Your father would have had to go to some city hospital to have the CAT scan, so Dr. Morse asked his friend to take him now. To be sure."

The three little words hung like a pall over them.

"Fletcher will feel so guilty," Margaret said after Desmond left in search of something for them to drink.

"Did you call him?"

"Not yet. He couldn't do anything. When we know how he is, we'll call." She squared and patted an already neat pile of papers in her lap and laughed. "Isn't it strange the things you do in an emergency? Before I left the house I ran up to the file drawer and brought Dad's medical folder and the insurance forms."

Cissy was amazed. "That's not crazy, Mom. That's fantastic. I can't believe how well you're doing."

"If Fletcher were here, I'd be leaning on him." Margaret sighed. "I just keep thinking about Poppa Barlow. His stroke left him so tragically disabled. All he could say was 'Bye-bye.' He said it for everything, but he thought he was talking clearly. He got so angry because no one could understand him. Dad wouldn't like that."

He'd hate it.

Desmond came back with soft drinks Cissy and Margaret took with them when they met Dr. Woodman. Immediately he led the way on a Dantesque search for an unoccupied space where they could talk. Finally he commandeered a table and chairs, setting up camp in the doorway of a storage closet.

"I've seen your husband, Mrs. Barlow, and I want to assure you that I think his condition is very good. He's conscious and has no severe pain. Just a headache and some confusion. Not bad." His elfin face was kind, and Cissy could see her mother instantly endow him with her complete, awed trust. She, however, held on to her misgivings and listened suspiciously to Dr. Woodman's plans for Joseph Barlow.

When Margaret had answered all the man's questions and handed over her records, they followed him to the curtained cubicle where Joseph rested. Cissy couldn't remember the last time she'd seen her father in bed. She was shocked to see how helpless and vulnerable it made him look.

And made her feel. If his own body could bring down the most powerful person in her life, what could hers, so much weaker, do to her? She glanced quickly at Margaret, needing the reassurance of her apparent calm.

After giving her father's cheek a kiss, she left her parents together and sought out Desmond. "I can't believe my mother," she breathed as she accepted his arm around her. "She's so calm. I thought she'd fall apart. She leans so much on Dad."

"Women usually are pretty strong in times of real stress. When Kevin was hurt Dad nearly went bananas. Mom was a rock though. Your mother doesn't surprise me. She seems a good person to lean on."

Cissy straightened. "I've never leaned on her," she said proudly. Then at Desmond's expression she qualified, "Well, not since I was little."

He smiled. "Everyone leans, Cissy. Even me." He did so then, almost toppling her over and making her laugh.

When Margaret came back to them Desmond insisted that they find a cafeteria where he put together meals for each of them. Margaret pushed salad from side to side on her plate while they tried to consume some of the unpalatable food. She gave Cissy a thin smile. "Fletcher should be here to see me now. I've always insisted that people eat to keep up their strength. He could laugh at me now."

"Did he call from Iris's?"

"We didn't expect him to. Your father was going to take over the presentation for Laird Chemical."

"Why not someone else? Aren't there other capable people in that company?"

Margaret sighed. "You know them. They *want* to do it all. I can't tell you how many good employees they've lost because neither of them would delegate responsibility. It's the main reason the company hasn't grown the way they say they want it to. They won't let go of even the dreariest details. Maybe now they'll have to."

Cissy nearly choked on her coffee at her mother's succinct summary of the company's management style. She ignored the knowing look on Desmond's face. Margaret went on ruminating aloud. "When I get home I'll call Tom Bennett and have him pick up the material for the presentation. Dad had it home to study tonight. Tom will be happy for a chance to shine."

Finished with their strange and strained meal, they made their way through the drab corridors to the Baker Building and another busy bank of elevators. Cissy trailed Margaret to her father's room and watched as she familiarized herself with all that it enclosed. Joseph seemed to sleep now, so after a few useless minutes she went to find Desmond. He wasn't in the crowded lounge, so she went on to the hub of the floor, the even more crowded nurses' station and reception area where the phone and loudspeaker vied for aural dominance. He was deep in conversation with two nurses. Her mother joined her before the conference ended and they were free to leave.

In the parking garage Margaret kissed Desmond, thanking him for his support and promising him a raincheck on their planned dinner. Cissy smiled weakly at the look he was giving her. Once he had tucked Margaret into the passenger seat of her car he said, "I'll see you when you get home."

"I may stay with Mom tonight." She felt vulnerable before his frown.

"Suit yourself," he said crisply. "I'll come by. If you're not there, I'll understand."

Cissy couldn't have said where her anger came from, but it bubbled up within her like liquid released from pressure. "You don't have to do that," she blurted out, her hand on the car door.

His hand covered hers and prevented her wrenching the door open. "I *want* to do it, idiot." He kissed her with more force than necessary at first, but he quickly gentled the pressure and opened the door for her. "Drive carefully," he said to her, and to Margaret, "Try to rest. The nurses said he should be fine. I'll tell Cissy the details tonight and she can relay them to you."

Cissy shut the door before he could arrange any more of their lives, trying not to show her resentment to Margaret, who would only lecture her about gratitude. Driving the big Chrysler took all her concentration as they bucked the Sunday evening traffic on Routes 93 and 128 from Boston to Lexington.

At home she felt useless as Margaret began the series of phone calls she considered necessary to keep the world and Barlow Security Systems on course without Joseph. Fletcher was notified by way of the Morgan family, who were keeping Joey and Phillip for their parents. Once

Margaret had heard her two grandsons talk about their trip to the zoo she was so cheered that Cissy felt her presence was no longer necessary. Rather than reinfect Margaret with her depression, she escaped to her Volvo and Boston. She couldn't make things worse for her mother, even to avoid Desmond.

She knew he would come by as he had promised, but she didn't expect to see him waiting on the top step of the hall, a paperback and a sack of penny candy entertaining him. If he noticed her resentful stare at his long form stretched across the landing, he chose to ignore it as he handed her the bag of candy and got up.

"How's your mother doing?"

"Fine. As you know perfectly well."

His arm pulled her into an awkward hug. He took the key and unlocked the door. "Be glad about it. Believe me, it's the best way, even if it does make you feel unneeded."

"I don't feel unneeded," she argued automatically. "Not really. I don't know. I'm just all mixed up."

He put a bag of groceries in her arms and ushered her into her own apartment as if she were the guest, not he. "You're hungry," he said. "You didn't eat up that roast beef your mother had been cooking, did you?"

"Are you kidding? Mrs. Millis next door came and took it home for her family dinner. Mom didn't want it to go to waste. Next week Mrs. Millis will bring an identical roast, baked to a turn, for their dinner. It was all worked out on some cosmic balance sheet before Mom left for the hospital."

Desmond grinned. "Women are practical."

"I'm not!" she said hotly.

"You're still a novice woman; they're in the big leagues. Don't take it so hard. Just because your mother didn't burn twenty dollars worth of meat, that doesn't mean she doesn't love your father."

"But he could have died!"

"But he didn't." His arms held her as indignant tears swept the room from her view.

Cissy couldn't understand her feelings. Not only did she reject everything Desmond said, she heartily resented him for saying it. She wanted to lash out at him, flailing and kicking, but instead she stood in the tight circle of his comfort, leaning and crying.

Thoroughly at odds with herself, she accepted Desmond's handkerchief and brought her sniffles to an end. "I thought my father was the last man on earth still using a cloth handkerchief," she said as he took it back from her.

"I don't like tissues. It's a holdover from childhood. Mom never thought we were dressed till we each had a handkerchief." He moved cautiously away, as if he expected to see her fall to the carpet without his support. Cissy straightened. "Why don't you go freshen up while I fix us something to eat."

In the bathroom Cissy saw why he'd made the suggestion. Her hair looked like a loose stack of straw and her eyes were red-rimmed to match the pink blotches on her cheeks. Only cold compresses and some judicious makeup restored her appearance, but it took Desmond's western omelette to offset her internal hollowness.

"I didn't think I'd be able to eat so much," she commented when she looked up from her whistle-clean plate.

"My apologies to your arteries for all the cholesterol, but I know how to cook only a few basic bachelor favorites."

She took in the ingredient-strewn counter and stove surface with a smile. "Well, in gratitude, I'll wash up,

Mr. Basic Bachelor." Desmond helped, however, and the kitchen was soon restored to normal, although the refrigerator now held twice its usual load.

"When does your roommate return?"

"Lorraine?"

"If that's her name."

"Either Thursday or Friday. She went to Michigan to meet her boyfriend's family."

"Do you work full-time tomorrow?"

"More or less," she sighed. "There are management seminars out in Newton every afternoon this week." She made a face. "Management by Directive. The Team Approach to Management."

"Will you be able to go to the hospital?"

"I'll go after work. Mom will be there most of the day."

"Meet me for an early dinner and then we'll go together."

Cissy inhaled deeply. "Desmond, you can't . . ."

He put his hand over her mouth firmly. "Don't tell me what I can and can't do, Cissy. I'm not infringing on your independence. I'm concerned, that's all. And unless you prefer to have me following two feet behind you, you'd better let me do it my way."

"What about what I want?"

"You're not in a position to judge right now."

"Desmond, I know my own mind and I don't want you taking over my life."

"Just dinner tomorrow night. You have to eat and so do I. Why not together?"

Why did it sound so simple when it wasn't?

"I saw a backgammon set in the living room. Do you play?"

She started to grin, then controlled herself and shrugged. "A little."

"A little?" His smile was as sly as hers. "Why don't we try it then?"

Their first two matches were warily played as both pretended a diffidence they didn't feel. Setting up the disks for the third time, Cissy offered casually, "Want to bet a little?"

"Why not?"

"Toothpicks or pennies?"

"Whatever you'd like."

"How about pennies, but we won't have to pay up. We'll just keep score in money for the fun of it." Cissy was confident. She knew Desmond had been holding back, but so had she, enough, she hoped, to be able to surprise him mightily. But it was she who was surprised. Four hard-fought games later she owed Desmond $285.50.

He ruffled her hair affectionately as she looked at the unbelievable total. "Don't let it bother you, Cis. I'll find a pleasant way for you to pay me."

"Pay you! You agreed we would keep score only for the fun of it!"

He laughed at her furious face. "And hasn't it been fun?"

She colored and finally laughed. "I'm a little bit competitive."

"Are you now? I'd never have guessed. Do you want to try getting it all back? One more game, double or nothing?"

"Would you let me win?"

"Are you kidding? Me, give up a hold like this over you?"

"Then, no thanks. I'll quit while I'm behind." She stacked the chips and folded the board.

"Smart woman." Before she could get up to put the set on the modular shelf, Desmond scooped her into his lap and began kissing her. "Twenty-eight thousand kisses, my sweet. You're my kind of gambler."

"You're not very flattering. A kiss should be worth more than a penny."

"Some are. That one was worth twenty cents, maybe."

She tried harder and soon he was groaning against her mouth. His response fed something primitive within her. She pressed aggressively against him, her stroking tongue deep in his mouth. His hands feathered over her back, then came to rest on her bare shoulders. She kissed her way to his ear. "I want you," she whispered. His hands tightened almost painfully, but he made no other response.

Cissy turned to swallow around the white-hot lump in her throat. Every muscle in her body was tensed, each nerve stretched on its skeletal rack. She could see only the underside of his jaw. She tried again. "Desmond, please. Take me to bed." How much plainer could she be?

His Adam's apple bobbed under the strain of producing a harsh laugh. "I don't want to wipe out your whole debt tonight, sweetheart."

She pressed on, entirely without pride. "I do." In spite of her wishes, his hands on her shoulders controlled her ability to move. She could feel his heart thudding against her breast and shoulder, and she could see the muscle jump in his jaw, but she couldn't see his revealing eyes until he released his grip. They were tormented.

"You really know how to hurt a guy, don't you?" he managed.

"Hurt?"

"Cissy, love, you're upset tonight. Don't you see? You're off balance emotionally. I can't take advantage of that and look at myself in the mirror tomorrow morning."

It took several long seconds for Cissy to grasp his meaning. He was refusing her. She had thrown aside caution and let him know in no uncertain terms that she wanted him, and he was refusing. Too incredulous to speak, she stared at him.

"Cissy, don't look like that. . . ."

"Like what?" She drew back, trying awkwardly to get off his lap. "I really thought you were different, but you're not. You're just like every other man in the world. It's got to be your terms or not at all!" Striking out in every direction, Cissy extricated herself from Desmond and ran to her bedroom to throw herself onto her bed. Humiliation choked her with tears.

When she felt the side of the bed depress she crawled as far as she could away from Desmond, but there was nowhere to go. He began to massage her shoulders. She wanted to protest, but there was no way. It felt so good. Comfort seeped around his firm hands, stealing away her tears. "Don't," she said once. He kept on until she was quiet. When he tried to turn her over to face him, she dug her hands into the bedding and fought uselessly. She wouldn't look at him until he caught her chin and turned her face.

"I wasn't rejecting you, Cissy. Tonight just isn't the time. Don't you see that?"

"I don't know what I see." She knew she sounded sullen and looked even worse than she had before dinner. She wanted to disappear, or at least be able to roll over and get away from his scrutiny. He leaned over her, his

107

weight propped on his left arm as he kissed a tear from her cheek.

"I don't want to hurt you."

Her lips trembled under his. "It did hurt though." She drew aside, looking up at his shadowed face. "How do you stand it?" For the first time she considered the male point of view. "I've done that to you. Doesn't it just kill you?"

He laughed. "Absolutely. That's why men have to have such inflated egos."

"I'm not without ego, you know. But I have nothing left now."

His chuckle lifted the damp tendrils of hair by her ear. He was stretched out beside her. "Sure you do. You'll be right back with another proposition any minute."

"Don't count on it, sport." She pushed back to regard him skeptically. "What are you doing here like this?"

"I'm comforting you." He pulled her back.

She snuggled. "This isn't a very good idea." She looked at him. "If you meant what you said."

He nibbled at her lower lip. "I've forgotten."

She nibbled back, then pushed him away. "I haven't."

He pulled her back for a deep, sweet kiss, then rolled to put his feet on the floor. "Okay, okay, I'm going." He touched her face lightly. "You okay?" he asked.

She nodded, smiling though his shadow probably kept it from him. "You're a great comforter."

"That's not all I'm great at," he said at the door.

"*That* remains to be proved!"

There was a moment of silence beyond the door, then Desmond chuckled and shut the outside door. Cissy stayed still in case he hadn't really left, then went to bolt the outer door. She was reading in bed when Desmond called nearly an hour later to set up their meeting for dinner and to relay the forgotten information about her father he'd gleaned from the nurses. As she drifted off to sleep she wondered about the strength of her physical attraction to him. Was it a good thing? Or would it just burn out and leave them strangers?

Cissy had just deposited her purse in the bottom drawer of her desk the next morning and was trying to unstick her blouse from the back of her waist when Mr. Pritchard's secretary told her he wanted to see her. She had to fight down her immediate sense of unease. He always made her feel like a truant called before the principal.

Without preamble he plunged into his message. Warren Blaisdell of the trust department wanted her to work for him. "He considers your background in economics ideal," Mr. Pritchard intoned, making minimal eye contact with her, as if he feared revealing his profound skepticism about her abilities.

"Does that suit you as well, Mr. Pritchard?"

He met her eyes then. "Oh, yes, Miss Barlow. I think we've done all we can in the loan department. We try for breadth in our training program. Exposure, you know." He got up. "You'll attend the seminars, of course, and report to Blaisdell tomorrow. I believe you have enough to occupy you today finalizing that survey on loan defaults."

"I'll have it on your desk tomorrow morning," she kept her voice demure but met his disapproving glance with composure.

Back at her desk she took several deep breaths in lieu of turning the cartwheels her body ached to do. Knowing she was free of Mr. Pritchard's heavy thumb gave wings to her thoughts and fingers. The report she'd procrastinated over would be done almost immediately.

With the report behind her and the evening with Desmond ahead of her, even the seminar leader's penchant for belaboring the obvious—"managers must manage in ways that facilitate work"—couldn't dim her inner glow. Only the nagging worry about her father could do that. Desmond had talked about left and right hemispheres of the brain, but what did it mean for Joseph Barlow? And had the damage been caused by a hemorrhage or a clot? Which was better? She'd have to ask him again tonight.

Tonight. She hugged the word to her heart all day and used it to will away the dregs of the muggy day. When she rushed into the cool restaurant from the bus stop it seemed to take forever before her eyes adjusted to the dimness enough to find Desmond. When he didn't immediately come forward to claim her, she approached him hesitantly. "Have you been waiting long?"

He half rose as she took a chair. "Forever." His eyes bored into hers.

From that moment on the evening was a blur. She barely tasted the food and later that evening even her mother's giddy delight that Joseph would be home in two days seemed no more than what she had known would happen.

"It was just a teeny-tiny hemorrhage somewhere in the right side of his brain where nothing very important goes on," Margaret burbled. "He has to lose some weight and cut down on fats and eat more vegetables and fruit. All those things I've been trying to get him to do. He'll hate it, but I don't care," she finished staunchly with a happy hug for Cissy and another for Desmond.

"Mom, are you all right?"

"Of course I'm all right. How could I not be?"

"Have you been here all day? You must be tired. Let me drive you home."

"No, no, dear, I'm staying right here. I forgot to tell you. Fletcher *and* Iris are coming here tonight. One of them will drive me home like you did last night. Oh, I appreciated that so much, dear."

"Have you eaten?"

"One of the nurses brought me a tray. They're so nice here. You go visit Daddy, then let Desmond take you home. You've both had to work all day. You must be exhausted."

Cissy escaped to her father's room and from there back to the smoky, crowded lounge and Desmond. Fletcher hadn't arrived yet, but his promise had been firm and Margaret couldn't be moved. She fell into Desmond's car and closed her eyes gratefully on the blurred lights of the passing city.

She roused with a guilty apology when the car stopped, looking from Desmond's shaded profile to the strange surroundings. "This isn't my street."

"It's mine. I have an air conditioner."

"Where is Kevin?"

"I slipped him fifty bucks to disappear."

"Desmond . . ."

"Just joking, honey. Like the phantom Lorraine, he's out of town."

"Lorraine is real."

"So is Kevin, but that's not the issue. . . ."

"Is there an issue?"

"I hope not, but if you think there is, I'll take you back to Beacon Hill."

Cissy laughed softly. "So damned noble."

"Not anymore." In the half-light of the streetlamp his

111

eyes glittered as he turned to look at her. "I used up my lifetime supply last night. No more Mr. Nice Guy here."

She touched his jaw. "Too bad. I kind of liked him."

He snapped at her fingers and when she drew them back reflexively he got out and escorted her inside. His hungry kiss stopped her from looking at the living room. When he drew back he said urgently, "I know you've had a rough day and you have to work tomorrow, but I want you to stay here tonight. I'll take you home in the morning and drive you to work from there. You can relax with a shower in Gwen's room while I grab a shave."

At her stunned expression he closed his eyes. "God, I'm killing it, aren't I?" he said softly. He pulled her back into his arms. "I'm sorry, sweetheart."

She laughed into his shoulder. "And to think I didn't believe you're an engineer."

"Now you know. Do you mind terribly?"

She straightened. "Actually, that shower sounds great, but come and get me before I have time to fall asleep, okay?"

He led her by the hand to Gwen's room and disappeared. She found a pretty peach-colored robe to wear and went along to the bathroom. When she came out, feeling nervous but refreshed, she found a glass of white wine waiting for her on the lighted bureau. She smiled and took several grateful sips before she hung her suit on the closet door. At his tap she called out, "Come in."

He wore a mahogany velour robe and a hesitant smile.

She raised her glass. "Thanks for the wine."

"You look beautiful."

"So do you." She walked closer, tipping her head. "You nicked your chin."

He didn't move. "My hand was shaking."

She fell into his arms. "Oh, Desmond, I've never met anyone like you. I think I'm in heaven."

His arms held her tightly. "Soon, sweetheart, soon."

CHAPTER EIGHT

He had promised so much. Heaven, no less, right here in his own bedroom with the Mondrian print covering the tack holes where his Red Sox pennant used to hang. It was his idea of heaven, Cissy here, but would it be hers? Could he make it hers?

He had tried. He had planned every detail this morning, the wine, the music on the stereo, the tinted bulb in the lamp. Then, perversely, he'd done his best to spoil it all. He'd announced his arrangements, letting all the seams show, and then, God help him, he had *towed* her here by the hand down the hall. She still had the wine, but he knew he'd never turn on the stereo; the light was enough of an obvious contrivance.

But, oh, he wanted to love her, to make her his. He sensed so much in her beyond her sweetness. There was hurt and confusion he wanted to wipe away, but more important, more essential to her, was the tender loyalty he knew she would be able to give. Loyalty like that, even stiffened by her innate pride and independence, would be the ultimate gift a woman could give a man.

She turned slowly in the center of the room. Smiling,

she offered up her glass for him to drink. He put it beside his and drew her into his arms.

"Your eyes look brown now."

"It's the room. All this relentless masculinity."

"You just happen to be looking at a twenty-one-year-old male's idea of what a bachelor pad should look like. Don't you think it should be preserved in a time capsule?"

"Along with my sweet-sixteen bedroom in Lexington. They could be a matched pair of fantasies."

"Is that still intact?"

"You know it is. Would my mother redecorate her only daughter's shrine?"

Desmond rested his cheek against her temple, bending a bit. "I can't believe this conversation."

"My nerves are showing." Her voice was low. "It would help if you'd kiss me."

Her mouth was soft and warm under his, familiar yet exciting. Kissing her helped him too. She melted against him, her arms around his neck lifting her breasts. Her silky robe was like skin, warm and smooth, molded to the sweet body beneath. When her mouth yielded to his fully he bent to place one hand under her knees, lifting her to the bed with him. The belted robe opened to her hip and he sat up to look at the pale sweep of her leg. He traced the edge of the peach cloth, the back of his knuckles lightly grazing her thigh.

"You are so lovely." He wanted to say more, but he didn't trust his voice. Her eyes were wide, shimmering and expectant, yet he had the feeling she might leap away at the slightest discordant move from him. He cautioned himself, slowly, gently. He pulled the belt apart and burrowed his hand between the layers over her waist. The heat of her skin as it touched his seeking hand sent a volley of desire rocketing through him. His hand spread over the arched bones of her ribs and she moved to fit herself to him, lifting her hands to his neck and turning into him.

"I'm not glass, Desmond. You can touch me. I want you to."

"I'm afraid I'll hurt you. You're so delicate. Your bones feel so fine."

"Fine and strong." Her hands pushed under the neck of his robe and pressed his shoulders.

He remembered their kiss on the beach and began to laugh. When she looked puzzled, he said, "Trust you to let me know what you want, Cissy love. I'd forgotten my too gentle kiss. I was doing it again, wasn't I?"

"Am I so obvious?"

"You need to be with me. It's just that you look like china. The light seems to shine right through your skin." He pushed aside the robe to look at her and was overcome as she also freed him to let their bodies touch. His control was too shaky to do more than hold her.

"I'm not china," she said, still insistent.

He kissed her neck, his tongue on the tender cord and pulse. "No, not china. You're too warm, too soft for china." He followed the slope of her chest to rest his face between her breasts as one hand coursed the length of her spine and cupped her firm buttock. She came alive then, twisting to press against him, her strong thighs gripping his.

Pushing her back onto the bed, he pinned her with his weight. He kissed her open mouth until she made a sound deep in her throat and trembled. He lifted his head slowly, watching until her eyes fluttered open and then he smiled. "Not china or glass, but not in charge here either." He saw the rebellion flare in her eyes and when she

116

started to speak he kissed her again until the tension in her body melted away. "I mean it. Don't rush me."

She started to stiffen, then went limp instead. "Yes, *sir,*" she whispered. She rounded her eyes in mock awe. "I'll just lie right here like a good girl and let you have your big ole way with me."

"Cissy." It came out between a laugh and a growl. "Damn it, I'd spank you if I thought it would do any good."

She squealed softly, "Oooh, now you're talking, macho man." Her wiggle was flagrantly erotic.

He began to laugh. "Will you please just shut up?"

Rubbing her foot slowly up the length of his leg, she challenged him with laughing eyes, "Make me."

Instead of laughing again, he kissed her. Incredibly, their exchange of nonsense had restored his usual sure sense of himself. Her response no longer threatened his control but fed it. He took fire from her kiss, from her hands around his back.

When she arched to offer the soft mounds of her breasts to his mouth, her cries of delight were almost a separate source of satisfaction. Her skin felt like heated satin over firm softness. He wet the surface for his fingers to slide over, memorizing what made her move or moan, what made her cry out.

In the light from the bedside lamp her body glowed, an erotic composition of peach and ivory made innocent by the pale strawberry blondness of her tousled hair. With her eyes closed she appeared to him withdrawn into a world of pleasure that somehow excluded him even when he knew it was his hand, his touch, his tongue, that had evoked the pleasure. He feathered the soft inside of her thighs and brushed the back of his hand between her legs, watching her face.

117

"Oh, Des," she whispered.

"Open your eyes, sweetheart. Look at me. I'm here too."

She laughed unsteadily and tried to focus on his face. "Oh, Des, crazy man, I know you're here. You're the reason I feel so good." She turned onto her side, pulling him down into her arms.

"You've never called me anything but Desmond. I like that."

"Crazy man?" she teased. "You're that and so much more."

He nipped her earlobe in retaliation. Cissy arched against him in an almost feline invitation. "Tell me what you want," he urged her. He felt he had to keep her talking, to keep her connected with him.

She smiled lazily. "You. I want you."

He stroked his fingers deep into her heated center. "Like that?"

She cried out, "Oh, God, Des!" Her head fell back as again her eyes closed.

He watched her struggle with her sensations as passion shook her. "Open your eyes, love. Let me see the way you look." She looked at him then, her eyes dilated and barely focused.

"Oh, please, Des." Her hands clutched his shoulders and slid down his back to pull him down onto her. "Now." His mouth absorbed her cry as their bodies joined, his hardness buried within her waiting softness. The motion implicit in her tightly muscled intensity nearly exploded at that moment, but he held her still for the requisite seconds and when he released his restraint she had softened again.

"So good," she said into his neck, where she buried her

face. When he began to move she looked deep into his eyes, joined to him emotionally as well as physically.

"I knew you'd look like this. Beautiful." It was his last intelligible sound. He could no longer hold back. The heat of her body, of her response, drove him into her again and again with fiercely possessive thrusts that broke his control into a million shards of light.

Cissy's arms ached from clutching Desmond for so long, but she wouldn't let go for a second of the long fall back into peace. She didn't want to breathe. She just wanted to keep Desmond with her forever.

"Precious," he whispered, trying to stir. "I'm heavy, honey."

She tightened her arms and legs. "Don't leave me."

He arched his back, breaking her hold to prop up on his elbows, but he stayed inside her as she wanted. "You are a gorgeous, wild woman, Mary Elizabeth Rose. I have no desire to leave you *or* your golden freckles."

Her chin came up sharply as she tried to push him off then. He didn't budge, but he did begin to stir inside her. He laughed at her surprised expression.

"Now look what you've gone and done," he teased, moving his hips against hers.

"You're faking," she accused, breathlessly fighting her own quickly spiraling response. A man couldn't . . . his kiss didn't let her think, nor did his hands. "Desmond McGinnis . . . oh, Des," she laughed helplessly into his shoulder. "I don't believe this."

At first his eyes reflected her amusement, mixed with an endearing, embarrassed pride, then the look of passion she had seen before banished all other emotions. His slightest touch sent her sensitized body into ecstasy and this time he was slow and excruciatingly tender. Wave after wave of pleasurable shocks washed over her, leaving her clinging helplessly to Desmond's enduring strength. She heard her cries from deep inside herself, recognizing her tears only because he kissed them away. She felt both broken and healed, riven and unified.

When Desmond released her at last, Cissy tried to roll away from him, but he shaped her to his side, making it easier to remain there than to achieve the separation that suddenly seemed so vital. Her tears had embarrassed and exhausted her. She couldn't think where they had come from, but they were still there, a fountain welling up within her, barely under control even now. Desmond's shoulder was wet under her cheek.

He pulled a sheet and light blanket from the bottom of the bed, tucking it around her before he snapped off the light. His hand found her face unerringly in the sudden dark. He stroked her hair from her forehead with tender fingers. His concern for her was like another presence in the bed. She tried to push away from him, but his arm automatically countered the move.

"Cissy, talk to me. Tell me what's wrong."

She shook her head, helpless to explain herself.

"Please, Cissy, don't shut me out. I have a mind and a heart. Give me a chance."

"I'm sorry. I just don't want to cry."

"It's all right to cry if that's what you feel. Have I hurt you?"

She took a shuddering breath that went a long way toward helping her regain her emotional control. Glad for the dark, she turned within his arms. "You haven't hurt me, Desmond. . . ."

"What happened to Des?"

"I don't know. I guess I didn't have breath enough then. I like your full name. It's how I think of you."

"Then I'll have an excuse to love you again so I can

hear you use my nickname." She didn't have to be able to see to know he was smiling. She could hear the smile in his voice and her mind, ever obliging, presented the illustration, unbidden. When she didn't speak, he urged her, "Go on. I won't interrupt again."

"This was a mistake, Desmond," she began carefully. "I shouldn't have come here. I shouldn't continue to see you."

"A mistake," he repeated flatly. Was he angry?

"I let myself get carried away. I can't afford that, Desmond. I have no room in my life for this kind of involvement."

"What kind of involvement is this, in your opinion?"

Cissy peered at his profile in the dim light, wishing now she could see his eyes. She'd never heard this tone from him. What on earth did it mean? The only time he'd been annoyed with her his voice had been carefully conversational, not dead. Was he hurt? She couldn't bear it if he were hurt. She touched the side of his face, the face he'd shaved for her. "Please, don't be angry. . . ."

He turned to her sharply, as if her touch had released some deep control. "Cissy, last night you wanted me. You *asked* me to take you to bed. You came here willingly tonight. What kind of game are you playing with me?"

Stung, she pushed back from him. "No game at all. I take full responsibility for being here. I did want you, but I can't handle it, that's all."

"That's all!"

"Desmond, you're a special person. You tear me up. I just can't take that. It's not what I want, not what I need now. Someday, maybe . . ." His hand caught her chin and held it.

"Tell me about someday," he muttered fiercely. "Tell

121

me why you cried in my arms the whole time I was loving you." He kissed her, giving her no chance to answer. It was just as well because although she couldn't have verbalized her thoughts, her answering kiss gave her away. It couldn't be helped. She could no more control her response to him than she could command the tide in Boston Harbor. In his ferocity Desmond had lifted her upper body from the bed to clutch her to his damp chest, but, assured of her response, he eased his hold. His mouth became gentle.

Cissy gloried in the change in him and nestled happily into his arms again. This was the real Desmond. He rolled onto his back, taking her with him in an untidy sprawl. He pulled her closer, his face warm on her neck.

Suddenly he lifted his head. "Cissy, my God. I forgot to protect you. I'm sorry. It just completely left my mind as soon as I held you."

She blinked in surprise, then laughed. "Heavens, you scared me." She relaxed against him again. "It's all right. I take birth control pills."

Desmond's arms remained tensed. "I see."

That voice again. She raised her head to look at him. "Do you?" she challenged. "Just what is it you see?" Her eyes were adjusted to the lack of light well enough now to see his tight expression. "I've taken the pill since I was seventeen, Desmond. Not because I'm promiscuous, but because I'm a runner. Do you have any idea what my normal mileage does to my body?" He was instantly contrite, but Cissy was too angry to care. "It's all right for you to do anything you want, to sleep with any female who's willing, to carry around your 'protection' in your pocket, but just let a woman . . ."

"Cissy, Cissy, please! You're right. I was out of line. I'm sorry."

"Talk about your double standard . . ." His hand on her mouth stopped her words.

"Sweetheart, don't. I know I wasn't fair. I just had this awful picture of you with someone else."

"You don't own me. Not now. Not ever."

"No one ever owns anyone else," he soothed. "I wasn't talking about ownership and I never would, Cissy. Don't be quarrelsome."

"Me, quarrelsome? What about you? You're the one with the cold, dead voice that cuts me to ribbons."

Incredibly, he laughed. "It cuts you to ribbons, does it? I'll have to remember that."

Cissy couldn't have explained the intensity of her reaction. "Don't laugh at me, Desmond. I can't stand that."

He lifted her above him, his hands on her waist, and settled her along his length. "It's either laugh at you or love you. One or the other."

His mood astounded her. "Then you'll have to laugh, I guess," she said. He began stroking her back and pressing her against his body. She drew back to look at him as he cupped her bottom. "You can't . . ."

"I thought we'd already established that I can. And I do. Now."

"Desmond."

"Make that Des," he said against her mouth.

Cissy woke alone, aware of a strange chill. Once she had identified the source of her discomfort, the air conditioner, she remembered everything—Desmond, his room, his lovemaking. She sat up and found Gwen's discarded robe, folded on a chair. Desmond's bathroom was a few steps away, but she went back to Gwen's, where her own clothes and assured privacy waited. She looked no more tousled than usual, but even as she inspected her face in the mirror for evidence of her night's activity, her freckles began to stand out in relief against her growing coloration. She addressed her reflection in annoyance, "Come on, Cissy, this is almost the twenty-first century. Blushes went out of style with buggy whips and long white gloves."

She took the ascot from her buff blouse and exchanged it for a narrow ribbon tie to change the look of her camel suit, just in case she didn't get home to change for work after all. She had learned to carry small extras of jewelry and scarves in her purse, not because she often spent the night as she just had, but in order to go out for dinner straight from work occasionally. She rehung Gwen's robe and carried her suit jacket, unsure where to find Desmond.

Downstairs, she walked soundlessly over the thick carpets, some richly colored Orientals, following her nose to the source of the breakfasty smells. Desmond turned at the click of her heels on the gleaming floor.

"Rats," he said, his fists on his narrow hips. His shirt was only half buttoned but neatly tucked into dark slacks.

"That's a fine greeting."

"I wanted to wake you up."

"I've been to that show," she said. "Avoiding that was my motivation."

He caught her into his arms. "I only hand out coffee when I want you to get up. That wasn't what I had in mind this morning."

His words and his encompassing warmth were already affecting her pulse. She laughed a little tightly, looking up into his warm brown eyes. "I'm not going to comment on that, lest you continue to feel challenged to prove me wrong—again."

Instead of laughing as she expected, Desmond peered at her earnestly and tightened his hold to keep her where he could see her expression. "Cissy, you're not a conquest. I wasn't trying to play the stud with you. Is that what you think?"

She hadn't intended to make a heavy comment, so it was impossible to respond to his searching question. "I don't know what I think." Why did he have to be so perceptive? "I wasn't being critical."

"I wasn't proving myself with you or meeting challenges or anything else remotely like that. Do you understand that?"

Her eyes dropped to his determined chin. She shrugged and tried to ease free. "It was no big deal."

It was the wrong thing to say.

His fingers dug painfully into her shoulders and she saw his eyes grow dark with fury before she could make a sound. "No big deal! Then what the hell was it to you anyway? Just a casual roll in the hay?"

"I meant the *remark,* you idiot!" She shoved against his chest. In his surprise he let her reel back from him, but when she tried to run from the room he picked her off her feet as if she were a small child. He carried her to a chair and sat down with her imprisoned on his lap. She fought with red-faced intensity, but he wouldn't release her. By the time she was quiet her blouse was untucked and he was laughing.

"I don't believe you," she spat at him. "You great, overgrown . . ."

"Prude?" he supplied.

"Yes. You act like an outraged virgin."

"Maybe I am."

"Ha!"

"I like you all mussed like this."

She slapped away the hand that tugged on the tail of her shirt and tried to get up.

"I even like you when you're angry."

"Well, I don't like you then."

"Then kiss me so I won't blow up again."

She took a deep breath to tell him off, then turned her head and said, "Something is burning."

"The French toast!" He jumped up, nearly dumping her onto the floor.

It wasn't burned enough to be inedible, thanks to a griddle with controlled heat, so they ate it anyway, letting laughter paper over the seams of their hypersensitivity to each other. She used the drive to Boston to tell him about her new job, what little she knew about it, and realized that for the first time in a long time she was looking forward to working.

The day didn't disappoint her. Warren Blaisdell was a breezy, informal sports fan who didn't let his sharp mind keep him from enjoying life. The Boston College hockey team was his pet, but his interest in athletics embraced all things physical. After they had reviewed the weekend sports news, however, he wasted no time. Cissy left his office carrying ten new portfolios to analyze. Warren—he insisted on the informal address—wanted recommendations from her as well as the usual evaluation of the worth of each new account and its holdings. The assignment neatly dovetailed with Cissy's interests and strengths.

Although the trust department seemed to outsiders less people-oriented than the loan office, to Cissy it offered a more positive service. Astute investment management provided not only the proverbial widows and orphans with needed income, but it also helped couples and young people build their capital reserves. If she did her job well, fewer people would be refused the home mortgages of the future. Warren promised she'd get a crack at all aspects of the department, from security analysis to interviewing potential customers. It was a heady challenge, one that at least kept her from dwelling on Desmond for a while.

The seminar topic for the afternoon, management styles for women, left her torn between indignation and hilarity. Only when she was heading home, however, did she decide to laugh. It was wrong, according to the male director, for a woman to attempt to manage either as a parent figure or as a good pal, both variants of time-honored male-management styles. Instead, the woman should forge a new approach, using her "unique people skills," and learn to lead by conciliation.

Before the group's leader could get around to defining that term, however, another trainee—male—had queried, "What about the woman manager as bitch?"

His mock innocence had been instantly accepted at face value, setting off the remainder of the session into a giant gripe session. Cissy hadn't seen its like since her dormitory days. She had sat, speechlessly waiting for the group leader to reclaim control over the proceedings. It never happened.

Instead, she and two other women were forced to listen to every form of tirade against women and women managers. That, or protest. After one woman twice tried to counter a complaint, only to be shouted down, Cissy decided to save her breath. She concentrated on fixing the details in her mind to relate to Desmond later. If only he would understand.

He did. As she picked at cold slices of onion that had fallen off their shared pizza, she wound down, ending her recital. He put on a grieved look. "How would you like it," he asked in a voice not much different from the ones

127

she'd heard all afternoon, "if you'd had this great tree house all to yourself and some *boys* came and tried to take over the whole thing?"

She couldn't help laughing. "The only trouble with that analogy is that the girls in my tree house couldn't wait to be taken over by the boys."

"But not you?"

She shook her head, her laugh fading. Damn him. Why did he always shift the ground under her feet like that? She forced some backbone into her denial. "No, sir. Not me."

He laughed, too much a gentleman to call her bluff in public.

In spite of his sympathy she didn't tell Desmond she'd gotten the last word at the seminar after all. It had taken careful timing on her part, but wasn't that part of the management game? Perhaps it was petty. Certainly she wished she'd been able to think of something pithier to say than "At least now a few women managers exist for us to talk about," but she *had* made a statement in rebuttal. She hadn't let the men off completely. Of that she was proud.

CHAPTER NINE

Cissy began to run again. Dr. Ferris had at last proclaimed her knee ready for reconditioning. The program he outlined was only mildly restrictive—no long runs, no speed work, no hills, no hard surfaces. Cissy should have been elated. In fact, she tried to be. She ran slow laps in the morning and returned to the track after work for more of the same. She continued to work out with weights, adding both weight and repetitions to her leg presses, enjoying only the massages that followed. But in spite of flogging herself into greater and greater accomplishment, she had no fire, no heart, and it showed when she ran.

With Desmond she allowed no hint of her discouragement to show. Which wasn't hard, really. When she was with him she put running out of her mind completely. With him she could be what she could be with no one else —a woman in love.

She hadn't confessed her love to Desmond, nor to anyone else. Her mother, of course, made the kind of grating, unsubtle comments that told Cissy she was not fooled by her daughter's studied indifference. Cissy ignored that.

She also tried to ignore the promptings of her own

heart as well, but without the same success. She didn't want to love anyone, much less a man like Desmond. But after a futile struggle she realized she could do nothing about her love for him except hide it. She would hide it from the world, if possible, but, at all cost, Desmond himself must never know. For him to know would mean destruction of all the independence she had painfully attained, as well as renunciation of the goals she had yet to attain.

For Cissy the answer was to compartmentalize her life into rigid, airtight units, each carefully maintained. Her job, finally satisfying, was one unit; running was another, less pleasing at the moment, but a source of promise nevertheless; and last was the rapture of loving Desmond.

And it was rapture. His touch was pure heaven. With his kiss he aroused deep hungers that only he could satisfy. No matter where she was she had only to think of Desmond to be flooded with delightfully alarming sensations. He was gentle and sensitive, patient and funny. She was hopelessly in love.

Hopeless too. Wrapped in her daydream, she had again gone one stop too many on the Blue Line past the gym. Resigned to the long walk back, she shouldered her way to the rear door with her duffel bag. It was all exercise, wasn't it? The way her workouts had been going lately she might as well be in it only for the weight loss. That, at least, had gone well. She had five fewer pounds to carry around the oval, for all the difference it made to anyone but Desmond. He, of course, protested the loss of each "round pound."

He was such a constant in her thoughts, even as she ran laps, that his actual presence by the door at first seemed unsurprising. But when he moved to stand by Lucky, Cissy realized she had not imagined him. He was really there. She ran on, grinding out the distance Lucky wanted, a confusing welter of conflicting feelings making her performance suffer. Her form, once so artless, deteriorated even more as she felt herself being watched by two such differing people with such disparate styles.

Seeing her run, Desmond would know she was stiff and mechanical. He would see her unhappiness. Lucky would see what he had observed from the beginning of her return to running, that her heart was no longer involved with her feet. He would blame Desmond. And her.

She concentrated on keeping Lucky and Desmond within her range of vision as she made her last turn. She was tired. Only postponing the ordeal of facing Lucky and Desmond at the same time kept her going. Then at the last minute Lucky walked away, leaving Desmond alone to greet her.

He put her warm-up jacket over her shoulders as if he did it every day. "This is a surprise," she commented.

"I found myself out this way and in need of a dinner companion. It seemed too happy a coincidence to ignore."

"I'll be another forty-five minutes here," she warned.

"That long?"

"I have to cool down, shower, and dry my hair. And I was going to grab a massage."

His grin broadened wickedly. "If I promise to take care of that last item later, could you put on some speed?"

"I could try." Her eyes devoured him. "Will you be here or outside?" The question was inane, only a way to keep from having to leave.

"One or the other." He turned her shoulders away. "Hurry it up."

She started away, then turned back. "What did Lucky say to you?"

He smiled. "Not a word."

She shrugged, moving away. "Well, he wouldn't, I suppose." Yet she knew Lucky would remember Desmond from the cape race. What did it mean that he failed to speak?

Over the next week and a half Cissy had ample opportunity to ponder Lucky's silence. Desmond came almost every night to watch her run, waiting without complaint to take her to dinner when she was ready. They often went to Lexington to visit her recovering father or to Brookline. She met Kevin. Desmond met Lorraine. As she ran she watched Lucky and Desmond watch her, feeling a surrealistic dread that did nothing to help her training.

Thursday Cissy felt stiff and her concentration lapsed. She slowed to a walk before her final turn, aware that all she had been thinking about was Desmond. He hadn't come. He hadn't promised, of course, but she had been looking forward to seeing him, counting on him not to disappoint her after a bad day. She walked slowly to the bleachers where her warm-ups were left.

This time Lucky didn't move away as she approached. She wrapped up in her jacket and put a towel around her neck, so wary the fine hairs on her neck seemed to stand on end.

"You were leaning," Lucky stated coldly. "Is that what Lover Boy tells you to do?"

Nonplussed, Cissy simply stared. She was used to his accusation that she was leaning. It was her natural running stance, a slight forward tilt of her body toward her goal that made her look eager in profile. Lucky believed the stance threw the runner's body out of alignment and destroyed, rather than enhanced, the power of the pelvis and legs. He and many other coaches advocated another stance, an upright position whereby the runner's body maintained a nearly perfect ninety-degree angle to the ground. Not to do so, as Lucky said over and over, meant the runner was turning a flat road surface into a hill, forcing the forward thrust of the legs to fight gravity as well as the road.

"I'm tired," she said quietly. "I always lean when I'm tired; you know that."

"Then try using the nights for sleeping for a change," Lucky growled.

"I sleep just fine, Lucky," she answered sharply. He was her coach and, as such, was entitled to comment freely on her performance, Cissy felt. But however much his position gave him a certain freedom, it was not license. She gave him a level look, waiting for his point. It would come, she knew.

"I suppose you think McGinnis has the answers, don't you? These boyfriends always do. He's not the first I've seen. A guy like that, just average himself, thinks he can pick up someone like you and ride to fame on your coattails. But it won't work, Barlow. He doesn't have it and you're a fool to listen to him. You're not getting better. You're getting worse. Your form has gone to hell. You just drag your carcass around the track, taking up my time and taking up space in my program. You can't have two coaches."

"I don't have two coaches!" Cissy couldn't believe her ears. "Desmond has never offered one word of advice. Not a single comment. Believe me, he has no intention of being my coach. He has enough to do."

"He looks busy." Lucky bit off the words.

133

"Well, he's not here now, is he?" she challenged. "Where do you get your ideas anyway?"

Lucky's eyes left her face and a slow smirk lifted the corners of his mouth. "Not here now?" He waved toward the entrance behind her.

Cissy didn't have to turn to know Desmond had chosen that moment to arrive. Too angry to speak, she simply walked to the locker room, ignoring the hapless Desmond as well as Lucky.

Cissy stood by her open locker for several minutes, her eyes sightlessly focused on its unremarkable contents. A heavy plastic bag from a local clothing chain specializing in jeans hung from a hook to hold her stockings and underwear, but her best summerweight gray suit and paler georgette blouse had to hang from a similar hook. The locker didn't accommodate the width of a standard clothes hanger. She folded the outerwear into her duffel bag, along with the stockings and slingback pumps. She would wear a denim wrap skirt and rose T-shirt home or wherever Desmond took her.

Desmond. Thinking of him made her remember why she was trying to dress to go home even before she'd done her cool-down stretches or showered. She banged the locker door and began the routine. The sting of the shower finally brought her face to face with the banked fires of her anger. It wasn't Desmond she resented, it was Lucky and his insinuations.

Incredibly, Lucky blamed Desmond personally for her failure to fall back into her old groove of excellence as a runner. She was supposed to be the best athlete Lucky coached. Before her injury she had been. But now?

The answer to that was as obvious to Cissy as it was to Lucky. Or to Desmond. Anyone could see she was running poorly, yet Desmond had said nothing to her about it, showing more forbearance than even her mother would have in his place. And Lucky suspected him of coaching her from the sidelines, of being responsible for her miserable running.

If only it were that simple. But the truth was that her malaise had little to do with Desmond. Its roots went back to her performance plateau before her injury.

Collegiate track had been a lark for Cissy. Her natural talent had won her a place on the team, a lot of friends, and a bit of glory—all immensely satisfying to a late-blooming tomboy. Then Lucky Edwards had spotted her at a meet. He told her father he could smooth the rough edges of her technique and enable her to fulfill her potential as a runner. He had a reputation as an excellent coach. He could also deliver the right job for a promising athlete, one that paid well legitimately, yet didn't demand all the precious hours in the day for training. Working only half time, she would be able to train seriously, both for the track and for a future job in the business world.

It had seemed so completely right. Like any talented person, she had been aware that her performance suffered from lack of commitment. Lucky gave her a chance to test herself on an absolute scale. She would throw aside her off-handed, slap-dash training, and with it the false modesty of pretending not to care about winning each race. She would become a champion.

Joseph Barlow had long talks with Lucky and with some of the people who sponsored his athletes. His honesty was unassailed. He was no *bonhomme*, but he was respected and he got results. Cissy grasped with both eager hands the opportunity he offered.

The first year had been wrenching. Once she was under Lucky's tutelage he began immediately remaking her, recasting her into his image of an Edwards runner. He scorned her natural talent as mere girlish enthusiasm and insisted that in all things she defer to his judgment. Autocratic to the core of his bones, he dictated the placing of each foot on the ground. Drills were endless, rewards few. Often Cissy's faith was shaken. Runners more senior than she were her only example that the hard work and self-abnegation would pay off. But finally it did.

Cissy turned off the shower and reached for her towels, one for her streaming hair, the other for her body. Her mind was far from this tiled refuge. She dried her hair automatically, one hand lifting the strands of limp hair, thankful no one else was there to intrude into her mental review. It was painful to confront her thoughts just now, especially with Lucky's words ringing in her ears, but the process, she feared, was long overdue.

None of her college victories had given her a reward to compare with her joy when she finally broke through for her first win as Lucky's star runner. It had taken so long to achieve, it had cost so much in time and effort, that the reward seemed sweeter because of it. And for a while that breakthrough fed her and led to others.

Now Cissy believed a different coach, different methods, would have fit her better. Although she did achieve, now she could see it shouldn't have taken so long. She should not have been forced to change everything about the way she ran, her stance, her footfall, her pace. Experience now reinforced what her balky reason had argued while Lucky had been remaking her. Runners were a varied lot and the best ones used technique to enhance their talent and natural proclivities, not to replace them. To run as Lucky would have her run, she had to concentrate on her form at all times, never give in to her natural gait and stance, never be herself.

To be sure, she had won as Lucky's robot, but not for

long. Then had come the performance plateau that had driven her to her injury. After the breakthrough she hadn't continued to improve even though she worked harder. She tried Lucky's sprint, but like everything about Lucky's advice it felt wrong. In rebellion and very much on her own, she had sought another way and found injury instead.

Now she understood the relief she had felt, and relentlessly repressed, when she first learned the extent of her injury. She had needed the time off from running to assess not only her goals, but the way she was going about their pursuit. During the recuperation period she had missed running. But not as much as she should have. Meeting Desmond had helped, but she knew he wasn't responsible for her second thoughts about training with Lucky.

If anything, falling in love with Desmond had distracted her from the course of reassessment she had begun early in her sidelined days. If she hadn't had Desmond to think about, she wouldn't be muddled still. She would know her own mind now.

She shut off the hair dryer and returned to her locker to dress. She pulled on her underwear and fit the skirt around her hips.

"Don't you want a massage today, dear?"

Cissy glared at Edna Edwards without attempting to modify her reaction. Edna was not Lucky, and Cissy had always sought to keep the difference in mind. It didn't help either of them for Cissy to transfer her anger at Lucky to his wife. Her life was undoubtedly hard enough. "I'll skip it today, Edna," she said finally, her tone more pleasant than her expression. From under her T-shirt she muttered, "Thanks," unaware that Edna hadn't turned away.

"I should tell you a story about Lucky," she said, surprising Cissy from arm's length. "I didn't hear what he said to you just now, but I know what's been on his mind lately, so I can imagine how it went, knowing my Lucky."

Edna was a spare woman whose weathered complexion and wavy gray hair, cut short, made her look timeless rather than aged. She had no children and tried to mother Lucky's runners as much as they and he permitted. Cissy had never availed herself of Edna's understanding, as much out of wariness as anything else. She didn't doubt Edna's sincere interest or her kindness, but she knew the bond between Edna and Lucky was unbreakable. She believed anyone who tried to stretch Edna's sympathy would only be hurt when the elastic rebounded. Whatever else she was, Edna was first of all loyal to Lucky.

"You know of course that long ago, in the dark ages, I was a runner too," Edna began. Her self-deprecation was typical, and so was Cissy's surge of impatience. Edna and Margaret Barlow elicited the same response from her. She waited for Edna to go on. "Lucky was my coach. I was his first pupil, but he wasn't my first coach.

"Coaching women wasn't very popular in those days, of course, but there were a few men even then who believed talent wasn't limited to males." Edna's voice was dreamy now, rather like a young girl's. "My coach was Hubert Lee, Bertie Lee, we called him. He was quite old-fashioned, courtly and proper, but very kind. I loved him like a child. When I met Lucky he was as irascible as he is now and he disapproved of just about everything Bertie had me doing. Training wasn't as technical then as it is now, but there were rules, especially for women. Lucky thought the rules were poppycock. He incited me to rebellion. It was easy, of course, because by then I would have followed Lucky into a burning building."

Cissy tucked her T-shirt into her skirt, the motion of her hands automatic. "So you're saying Lucky sees himself in Desmond, is that it?"

"Let's just say he's aware of the possibility. It's happened before."

"But Desmond isn't interested in taking over. He hasn't said anything about my training. I told Lucky the same thing."

Edna turned away then. "I just thought it might help you to understand. You are important to Lucky, you know."

Cissy could think of nothing to say. She knew she was important to Lucky, but not why. Or rather, she did know why, but the knowing wasn't enough. His caring wasn't the kind she could relate to. Yet for him to be jealous of Desmond? It gave her pause.

She closed her locker and went to find Desmond. This time he was talking to Karen. Would Lucky read an ulterior motive into that as well?

"Aren't the stars beautiful?"

"Um-hm." Desmond propelled the glider with one idle foot. His other bare foot rested beside Cissy on the cushioned seat. From her place between his legs she could feel his thigh flex with the slight motion.

"One time when I was holding my nephew Joey on my lap at night he started to count the stars. He'd just learned the numbers to ten, so when he got to ten he started over again and again. He was amazingly patient. Then he gave up and said, 'Oh, so many stars!' I'll never forget the wonder in his voice." She felt him remove his

139

chin from the top of her head to kiss the abandoned spot, and she sighed.

This was paradise. Tomorrow Kevin and his girlfriend would come, then Mr. and Mrs. McGinnis would return from San Diego, and Gwen from wherever she was. But right now it was Friday night and she and Desmond were alone with the stars. The only sounds were the muffled swish and thump of the ocean well below the porch, punctuated by the squeak of the glider. Desmond's left hand offered his Tom Collins and took it away when she shook her head. His right hand covered the zipper on her shorts. Against her back, his chest lifted in a deep, answering sigh.

"Want to walk on the beach?"

"I don't want to move ever again." Getting to this moment had involved so much work—the drive, dinner, a shower before she could change into this well-worn shorts set.

"No?" His thumb lifted the tab on her zipper.

"Well," she laughed.

"Come for a run on the beach with me in the morning." Although there was no command in his voice, it was a suggestion, not a question.

She groaned. "I'm going to sleep late. Besides, I can't run on the beach. Too much strain." It was true. Hard surfaces were out according to Dr. Ferris, but so were too-soft surfaces. On sand the heel could sink too deeply and strain the delicate balance of her still sensitive tendons.

"Okay, then we'll run on the golf course. That surface is just right, Goldilocks."

He had her trapped. "Don't be a nag. I don't want to run. I want to sleep late."

"I'll wake you up so nicely, you won't mind at all. It'll be fun."

"You and your coffee? Or would it be juice?"

"Neither."

Cissy smiled and turned her head to nestle into his chest. "Okay, you can wake me up. But when you go to run, I'm going back to sleep."

Desmond heard her determination, but his own was greater. Until last week he had never seen Cissy run except in his imagination. He had known, however, that she would run with all the power and grace he sensed coiled within her body. After all, her fluid motion had wrung praise even from jaded sportswriters. So, although he was a little put off by her apparent lack of enthusiasm when she began training again, he was totally unprepared for the runner he finally saw circling the track at the Colonial Club. This stilted, thumping creature was Cissy Barlow?

He went to see her nearly every day, always hoping this time he'd see the real Cissy run. Even making generous allowance for the aftereffects of a major injury, he knew what he was seeing was an abomination. When she didn't say anything, despite her obvious unhappiness, he knew the problem was acute.

What he didn't know was what to do about it. Part of him accepted that it was her problem, not his. She was proud and independent. If she didn't want to talk about it, he had to respect that. He could make himself available to her on every level, but if she still said nothing, what could he do?

So he pondered and waited, watching her robotic drills and her stoic indifference even to the subtle pressure Lucky exerted with his morose observation from the sidelines. As he waited, Desmond questioned his own mo-

141

tives as well as hers. Why was he concerned? Was he perhaps being as heavy-handed as Edwards? She hadn't asked his advice, and, anyway, what did he know? He was no coach. She hadn't complained. She hadn't even asked him to come, although once he started she seemed relieved to see him.

Except yesterday. Yesterday a lot of things had changed, including his own policy of neutrality. Yesterday he saw, finally, a spark from Cissy. It was only anger, but it was a start. He didn't intend to let the spark die. He wanted to see Cissy restored to herself as a runner of passion and fire. Getting her to run with him in the morning was the first step. As with all first steps, it involved a certain risk, but he would chance falling on his face rather than stand idly by watching her spirit die.

Cissy rested her ear over Desmond's steady heart, turning to lie within his arms. One leg trailed down beside his and bumped Jock. She sat up. "I didn't know we had company." Sensing that he was being addressed, Jock slowly rose as if he were being propelled upward by the agitated action of his tail against the floor.

When he began a mournful howl, Desmond complained, "Haven't you ever heard of letting sleeping dogs lie?"

She patted the russet head and stood. "He just knows it's time to check over the hedges before bed."

Desmond started up. "Okay, okay."

"You stay and finish your drink. I'll go with Jock." She was strangely relieved that he resettled on the glider, content to let her go by herself. She wanted a few minutes away from him. Why? Because he was getting too close? Nonsense. With Desmond she didn't want the kind of barriers she erected to keep others away. Still, he was pushing on her neat compartments.

142

Cissy walked to the edge of the lawn, her eyes on the phosphorescent meeting of sea and sand. Behind her, Jock's ID tags jingled, stopped, then resumed as he investigated the dewy yard. So what if Desmond asked her to run with him? she argued. Lucky would see it as the opening of a pitched battle between them, but why should she let his suspicions poison her mind? She knew Desmond.

Cissy shook her head and stretched. She didn't want to think anymore. Consciously, she watched the curl of a wave, forcing air from her lungs as the wave died. A piercing whistle broke into her concentration as Desmond called the forgotten Jock back to the house.

"Come on, miserable hound," Desmond scolded affectionately. "Time for bed."

Cissy started to turn toward the darkened porch when he whistled again. She froze. "I didn't hear that. I know I didn't," she muttered, hands on her hips.

Desmond's voice carried as easily as hers had. "It's a special sound only dogs and certain women can hear. Beautiful women," he amended quickly.

She knew he was laughing, but she walked forward with great deliberation. "Desmond McGinnis, this is one gaffe you can't sweet-talk your way out of. You do *not* whistle for me."

"You whistled for me once. I loved it."

"That was encouragement."

"So is this." He stepped from the shadows and swung her up into his arms. "It looked to me like you were avoiding me, and here I am, your biggest fan, no matter what you do."

He carried her through the dimly lighted house, sure-footed on his own ground. His line of patter kept her off-guard and amused, in spite of herself. "Who would have

143

believed I'd end up smitten with a reformed loan shark? One who's now bleeding the life savings of widows and their poor little children for corporate profit?"

Cissy couldn't control her giggles. He'd actually run up the lighted hall staircase calling himself "smitten." They were at his bedroom door before she could manage even a poor response. "I'd rather bleed you!"

"Argh!" he cried. "Leeches!" And dropped her onto the bed so hard she bounced.

"Desmond, you are a certifiable nut."

"But look what it got me," he countered reasonably. "Here you are in my bed, right where I want you. No fuss. No argument."

"You're smug, self-satisfied . . ."

"And a whole lot worse."

He kissed her gently, his warm mouth so sweet Cissy drew back quickly. "Desmond . . ."

"Don't think so much, Cissy." He took her hand and put it over his heart. "Just feel for a while. It's all right. Feel my heart. You make me feel like that. Trust it. Trust me."

CHAPTER TEN

What could she do? All her bright remarks about his pulse being caused by carrying her up a flight of stairs died unspoken. Her own heartbeat quickly accelerated to surpass the jackhammer pace under her fingers. She could feel herself begin to melt toward him in yearning. His beautiful dark eyes caressed the curves and hollows of her face like warm fingers.

"Why is it so hard for you to let me love you?" he asked softly.

Cissy choked out a small laugh. "It seems to me I've done nothing else since I met you."

"What else have you wanted to do?"

"Nothing. That's the problem." She put her cheek against his shoulder, her mind deliciously blank as his hands slid up and down her upper arms.

"Now all I have to do is get you to see that's not a problem. It's the way it should be." He lifted her chin to look into her eyes. "Right now this is all the world that counts. Just the two of us."

His mouth took her parted lips and the world went spinning away into darkness and unreality. All that mattered was within the pool of light falling from the hall onto Desmond's bed, part of a wide circle encompassing the tight circles of their arms around each other. His lips brushed hers lightly, tasting and sampling without greed.

His restraint tested Cissy's patience. She didn't want this gentle wooing and winning by inches. She flicked her tongue into his mouth, rewarded for a moment by the tightening of his body. When he didn't pursue her invitation she ran her hands down his spine and pulled his T-shirt free to give herself the run of his back. Her nails dug lightly into the cleft of his vertebral column, burrowing below his beltline. His kiss began to change. She pushed up the T-shirt and he released her to take it off, rising to his knees. Immediately she unhooked the belt of his tennis shorts and lowered the zipper. She pushed down the shorts and briefs, not willing to release him until he was lying back on the bed naked. The light fell on the curling hair of his chest and arms, releasing its fiery undertone to contrast with the rest of his intriguing darkness. She wasn't entirely aware of the way her eyes were devouring his exposed body until he said with an exaggerated sigh, "Oh, the life of a sex symbol."

She laughed then and met his amused glance. "Complaints from the one who kept urging me to open my eyes?"

"Would it matter if I did complain?"

"Right now, I don't think so," she admitted honestly. "I'm enjoying myself too much." She ran her fingertips in a line from his thigh to his shoulder and back, making only one detour to circle his navel lightly. She watched his face. "There's a wonderful sense of power in being the clothed person, isn't there?" she mused.

When she bent over him to let her mouth and tongue repeat the journey he caught her shoulders in his hands. Strands of her hair trailed along his length, making his muscles flex sinuously. He took a sharp breath, his hands hard on her arms. "Enjoy your power and your clothes while you can," he warned tightly. "They won't last much longer."

She reveled in the beauty and power of his body. He was hard, yet giving and supple; his skin was warm and smooth across the abdomen, tufted with crisp hair on his chest. She gloried in the fact that she could make him writhe and twitch with desire.

Then his hands were under her T-shirt, shaping her unrestrained breasts and drawing her up to his face. She offered no resistance as he pulled the garment over her head to nuzzle and fondle her fullness, glad there was no bra to interfere. Now she wore a bra only for work and running. His hands were warm, his mouth hot. She arched against him, hearing only distantly that he called her soft and beautiful. She poured herself over him, reluctant to endure the small moment of separation he needed to take off her remaining clothes. Why had she wanted them on so long?

Desmond rolled quickly to reverse their positions and claim her mouth in a hungry kiss. There was no more languor in him. His tongue invaded her mouth with promising thrusts. She wrapped her arms around his waist, pulling him to nest between her legs. When he drew back to look down at her she didn't open her eyes. He kissed the lids, moving down over her cheeks and neck to her breasts. When his loving attention there made her move restlessly, he slid lower, easily breaking free of her embrace.

Cissy wound her fingers into his hair, kneading and clawing his scalp. "Des, oh, please," she whispered. His hands were firm on her hips, holding her for the tender torment of his lips and teeth. He nipped, then licked, the

147

inside of her thighs, with each touch coming closer to her heart.

The entire galaxy exploded within her in radiating circles of heat then, as his mouth took possession of her womanhood. She tried to form words, but they dissolved into small sounds she couldn't control. Pleasure made her weak and incoherent. She moved in supplication, in protest at unbearable delight, and finally, when she could stand it no longer, he filled her with his thrusting power and heat.

"Oh, Des*mond!*" she cried out as they joined. She bit her lower lip in an effort to control her spiraling emotions. She didn't want to cry again.

He caught the look and froze.

She clutched his tensed buttocks, arching toward him.

"I'm hurting you. . . ."

"No, no, don't stop. Please, don't stop. I . . . just feel so good," she finished with a rush.

"Oh, you do, sweetheart." For a while his pace was slowed, but the momentum soon crested as they drove to meet each other in complete accord, each giving, each taking in abandonment.

"Oh, my love, my love." Desmond's words or her own thoughts? She clung to his slick body with muscles that only clenched, refusing separation.

"You're biting your lip again, Cissy my heart."

She smiled at the term. "Where do you get those expressions?" It was an idle question, not one she expected him to answer.

He propped on his elbow to look at her. "From the Blarney Stone, of course. Do you mind?"

"Of course not. I love it?"

"What else do you love?"

The word *you* popped into her mind. It would be such

a relief to say it, but she didn't. "I love the way you make me feel, Desmond my heart. And lots of other things as well."

"After the way you said my name this time I guess I won't complain any more about having no nickname from you."

Cissy blushed even as she laughed. Then her color deepened when he noticed it and said, "I'm glad you can still blush. That means there are ways I can shock you yet." He settled onto his back and hugged her to his side, where she nestled. "You still haven't explained why you kept biting your lip, you know."

"Do I have to?"

"You know you don't."

"Would you have preferred to have me cry?"

"That would depend on why you cried."

Cissy shifted her head to see his face. "Sometimes I cry when I'm especially happy."

His arm tightened. "Then you can cry." His smile was like a gift only she could receive. He smiled to himself, unaware that she could see his pleasure. In an instant the pleasure had become contentment and peace. His sigh was deep. "You make me especially happy, Mary . . . Elizabeth . . ."

Cissy waited for the Rose, but it never came. Desmond was asleep. She stayed very still, watching the rise and fall of his chest. Far from feeling cheated by his drift into sleep, she felt it as a benediction. His arm still held her. When she reached to pull up the covers, he stirred in protest. She moved back into his embrace before he could wake, her last thought gratification that she hadn't disturbed his rest.

In the morning he gave her no such consideration, however. An annoying tickle on her arm first broke into her peace. She slapped at the spot and rolled away to wrap her arm under the sheet. The sheet resisted her tug. She flopped onto her stomach, but there was no escape. The fly moved to her back. She wiggled, pushing herself lower under the covers, and opened her eyes.

Desmond.

"You rat," she groaned. "Go away."

"That's not what you said last night."

"I'm not responsible for last night." She raised her head enough to glare at him. "Anyway, you owe me this morning because you fell asleep on me last night. Right in the middle of my name!"

"If you had the right number of names, that wouldn't have happened."

Cissy pulled the pillow over her head to escape. Why did he always have a snappy comeback? She half expected him to snatch the pillow away from her, but he didn't. Instead, he pulled down the sheet and blanket. Her grab for them was much too late.

"What was it you said last night about the power of being the person wearing clothes?"

"I hate you, Desmond McGinnis, now and forever." She didn't have to look at him to know he was dressed for running.

"That's progress," he said calmly. "At least you're talking about forever."

He straddled her legs and began massaging her back, his strong fingers moving expertly on her shoulders. Cissy had to work to keep from groaning out loud as every trace of annoyance slipped away from her. His hands moved slowly down her back, kneading the smooth flesh his knees embraced.

"Desmond . . ."

Suddenly he swung away with a strained laugh. "I

think what we're about to do here is demonstrate the power of the *un*clothed person." He stalked across the room, grabbed his robe on his way out, and tossed it carelessly to Cissy.

She sat up and pulled on the robe, too awake—that was the tactful word for her condition—to go back to sleep. She hadn't intended to run with him, but the crisp mix of sunshine and sea air pouring through the window was as irresistible as Desmond himself.

He was almost curt when she appeared in the kitchen, giving only a nod to acknowledge that she was dressed for running. She drank the glass of orange juice he offered and followed him out to the car. By the time they reached the golf course his disposition was restored and he took her hand walking from the parking lot. Pleased, Cissy actually skipped several times, not even thinking that she might look childish.

Desmond noticed, however, and silently applauded. Happiness, it seemed to him, was what was missing in Cissy's running. It was what he hoped to show her this morning. Seeing the brightness in her eyes as she took in the undulating greens before them, he was thankful the day had cooperated with his plan.

Cissy squeezed his hand. "This is so beautiful, Des. Is this where your father plays golf?"

"And my mother. She's one of the best women in the club. Dad's really only a duffer. For him it's an excuse to be outside; Mom is good."

Cissy absorbed that information without comment, trying not to let her surprise show. She was ashamed of the assumption she'd made. She, of all people, should have known better. She concentrated on the rough outline of a scrub pine, vivid against the groomed slope of grass, until she felt she could meet Desmond's perceptive

151

eyes. She was absurdly relieved to see no censure in him. She wouldn't have been as charitable, she knew. Why did she bristle so over every little slight while he didn't? Because she was female?

"How about it?" he asked with an expansive wave before them. "We have the place to ourselves for an hour at least, longer if you don't mind playing dodge 'em with the golf balls."

"An hour will be plenty, but I have to do a few stretches first." She picked out a tree to lean against, strangely self-conscious until she realized Desmond was doing the same thing nearby. Then the routine claimed her and she forgot him. Embarrassment flared again when she finished and found him waiting, but as he loped off she followed at a careful jog.

At first Cissy watched Desmond run, not even thinking about herself. It was easy for her to lose herself in admiration of his strong, muscled legs and back. His dark forest green shorts trimmed with gold set off his burnished skin and hair as if they were designed just for him. Once she was warmed up, however, her conscience took over and she began to think about form. Lovely though the setting was, this was still running—something she was serious about.

Desmond turned to look at her, then reversed his body to run backward. The action startled her and she nearly tripped on her own feet. "Don't do that," she protested. "How can I concentrate watching you run like that?"

"Don't concentrate. This is just for fun. *You* run backward and let me chase you."

"Idiot. You want me to tear up my knee again?"

"Of course not. If you don't want to try that, then race me to the other side of the green."

She shook her head. Racing was out.

"Have you ever done *fartlek?*" he persisted, still running backward just in front of her.

"You mean intervals, don't you?" It wasn't her favorite thing to do, but of course she had done it—endlessly. The term was a Swedish word for timed speed drills of varying lengths and intensity.

"No, not intervals—*fartlek,*" he insisted.

"Same thing," she argued. Then she stopped and glared at Desmond. "What is this, a quiz?"

He reversed direction without missing a beat and stopped in front of her. "No, it's not a quiz, Cissy, but neither is *fartlek* the same as intervals. It's not a drill, just a way to have fun. With *fartlek* you just run the way you feel for a period of time, slow or fast, whatever your body tells you it wants to do just then. It's a way to get in touch with your body and learn to listen to it rather than follow a prescribed pace the way you do with intervals. It's perfect for a day like this on a golf course. It's like being a kid again and running just for fun."

Was he being too insistent? Her chin was stubbornly set, but he thought he saw a small gleam of interest in her eyes.

"Lucky uses the terms interchangeably."

"A lot of people do," he dismissed. "Want to try it? You just do what *you* feel like doing. Run your own pace, your own way. No rules. That's the only rule."

She hesitated, drawn to the picture he was painting.

"We'll take this green. You choose. You can circle first, then run up and down the crest, or do it the other way. Whichever you do, I'll take the opposite. That way we won't influence each other or get in each other's way."

Cissy shrugged and said with a diffidence she didn't feel, "I'll go around first. I haven't done even a mild grade like that for a long time."

Desmond matched her feigned indifference. "Okay. Just remember, listen to your own body. Stop when you feel like it." His hand swiped at her hair in an affectionate gesture of dismissal that somehow tossed a challenge at her too. Then he ran off toward the slope while she began to jog the circumference of the lush surface.

She couldn't help but watch Desmond's approach to the top of the molded rise. His pace slacked, becoming slower and slower as the hill crested; then he swooped like a bird down the other side. She laughed out loud and veered toward the hill. She made a slower ascent, spiraling toward the top for a while before she pumped her arms and powered up the slope.

It had been so long since she'd run up a hill that she felt an almost giddy sense of achievement. Knowing that Desmond was as aware of her as she had been of him, she broke into a "Rocky" dance of triumph on the top. With anyone else she would have felt foolish, but with him she felt only free and happy and wonderful. When she heard him laugh she began to run down the opposite side from where he circled. She ran with great care then, for the downhill could tear her knee badly. For that she listened hard to her knee, relieved that it issued no protest.

When she saw him running toward her around the perimeter she opened her arms wide as if she would fly into his embrace. She saw his grin and veered just enough at the last minute to sail past him, her arms still flung out, laughing so hard she had to stop running.

She threw herself onto the soft grass, still laughing, and rolled to a stop. When had she last felt like this? She stretched her arms wide to embrace the clear blue sky. What she could see, the rolling green ground, the perfect circle of the sun, had the simplicity of a quilt design, each element separate, as if outlined by invisible stitches.

She felt Desmond's approach before she heard his foot-falls against the muffling grass. He threw himself down beside her, breathing hard. He didn't touch her or speak and she wondered as she had so often before how he had achieved his sensitivity. "How is it you know so much?" she asked without moving. She hadn't planned her words. They popped out, the product of an unguarded moment in her life, like so many with him.

She rolled over onto her stomach quickly and propped on her forearms to look at him, afraid he'd offer a quip. "Really. An honest answer, Des. What is it with you?"

"I can answer that only by admitting to a lot of feel-ings you're not ready to hear about."

He didn't look at her, but her panic was suddenly a living thing between them. He loved her. She knew it as well as he did, but to have him allude to it terrified her. She didn't want it spoken. If he said it out loud, they'd have to deal with the implications and all the sweetness between them would melt away into acrimony.

But he hadn't said it, and although the moment stretched unbearably under the weight of the unspoken, it remained only a skipped heartbeat in real time.

"I had a totally selfish reason for this morning. I wanted to see the real Cissy Barlow run. I knew the woman I'd been seeing at the track was, I don't know, a wind-up doll maybe? Not the real thing anyway."

Cissy let his words fall into a vacant part of her mind. She didn't want to consider them. He wasn't looking at her, so she was free to study the strong planes and angles of his face.

"What do you think about when you look at me that way?"

Surprised, she answered honestly. "That you scare me. You're so sure."

"Sure?" He sat up and wrapped his arms around his knees. "I wish I were, honey, but I'm just like those guys in your management seminar. It's more than half bluff. The less I feel sure, the more I act sure."

"*Now* you tell me the secret of male success." She got to her feet. "Why don't we run some more?"

Squinting against the sun, he looked her up and down. "Well, I know the secret of your success—work and great legs."

When he caught up to her so they could run side by side she said, "Running outdoors is so different. I'd forgotten how nice it can be. I think I've just become sour going round and round the track. I don't know if I can face that place again after this."

It was a thought she held through the weekend and Monday at work, but she forced herself back to the track. Saturday morning with Desmond she had rediscovered the joy of running. Now she was determined to hold on to that joy and make it the heart of her program.

But it wasn't easy. The track felt oppressive, confined. She had to call on her reserves of mental toughness and imagination to put herself back onto the golf course. Just ahead of her she conjured the image of Desmond's loose stride and tried to match it. She pushed aside her nagging conscience that carped about form and let herself go, leaning into the turns. It began to work.

By Wednesday she was on a roll. For the first time since her injury her workouts lifted her spirits, even without Desmond, who was away on business. Lucky ignored her, as did Karen and Allison. She noticed, but did not veer from the course she had set on Monday. Her own body told her she was right. What better authority had she?

Desmond's calls were another source of pleasure for

her, though they were harried and sometimes almost impersonal except when he told her about Moira's new son. He didn't ask about her running and she volunteered nothing. He would return Thursday in time to take her to Cotuit again for the Labor Day weekend.

Although the family reunion on Sunday was billed as the high point of the weekend—indeed, of the summer—Cissy found herself dreading the prospect of so many McGinnises in one place. Like the Queen of England, Desmond's grandmother always celebrated her birthday on an official day, this year Labor Day Sunday. Desmond implied that more than her natal day was suspect in the arrangement and that perhaps she wasn't actually eighty-four yet either, but he said it all with a laugh.

Meeting Moira loomed as still another hurdle to Cissy in a weekend sure to be full of tricky moments. Moira's approval of her would be important to Desmond. He made automatic comparisons between them so often that Cissy knew they were neatly bracketed in his mind as similar people. Yet how could she relate to a new mother and an apparently ecstatic young wife? And why should she even want to?

The answer to that question was as disturbing as the butterflies Cissy carried to the cape under her belt. She loved Desmond. She admitted the fact freely to herself, if to no one else. She loved his family, both as an ideal and in reality, but her coming confrontation with masses of McGinnises frightened her more than she cared to contemplate. She would be on trial. She was ambitious and independent, not likely to fit the mold of a McGinnis woman. How would they react to that?

Friday night she met Boyd, the brother Desmond introduced as "the family's only weirdo" with obvious pride that belied his words. At twenty-one, Boyd was taller than Kevin or Desmond, with traces of adolescence still clinging to his lanky frame. His ash-blond hair was unfashionably long, but the style helped soften his craggy features. Cissy saw him as a troubadour in a cloak and feathered hat. He bobbed his head to her with a shy grin, accepting his brother's ribbing with a grace that told Cissy he was every bit as securely himself as Desmond or Kevin.

Over a plate of lasagna he told Cissy he had earned his label by writing poetry and music. "I'm even an English major," he laughed, "so when I graduate I'm going to come home and sponge off Des and Kev. They're going to be my patrons."

She also met cousins of both sexes, many of whom were going to sleep in Gwen's loft with them. Naturally Moira's room was reserved for her family, but that night she didn't appear to claim it and Cissy preferred not to ask about her lest someone think she was unhappy about being with Gwen and the cousins.

She wasn't. In fact the evening flew by like the best party Cissy had ever attended. One contingent had been sent earlier to scour the beach for driftwood, ostensibly for the next day's cookout, but soon there was a bonfire that pulled everyone to the circle of leaping flames. People swam, threw Frisbees and footballs, then drew near to listen first to Boyd's songs, then to Kevin's ghost stories.

Cissy sang along softly and shivered with delight in the security of Desmond's arms. He bent his head to whisper, "If you have any nightmares, I'll only be a shout away downstairs."

"Are you kidding? No self-respecting nightmare would dare come near the loft."

His chest lifted in a sigh. "I wish it were last week." He kissed her forehead and moved his hand restlessly over

158

the meeting of her jersey and shorts. She stirred and he laughed shortly. "Tomorrow night wear a big loose sweater, okay? I'm going crazy not being able to touch you." He nuzzled her ear. "Let's sneak out and find a motel," he groaned softly. "Or a backseat. I'm desperate."

Cissy was glad for the play of shadows and flame that hid her instant response to Desmond. Her frustration equaled his, but she didn't acknowledge it. In the next moment she was glad she hadn't, for Boyd met her glance and conferred a huge wink on her. She straightened as unobtrusively as possible and nudged Desmond back to reality. He rolled his eyes expressively but rejoined the group.

It was midday before Moira and her family arrived and already Cissy was exhausted. She had jogged with Desmond, helped Gwen set up picnic tables, and collected firewood with Kevin. Neil played the attentive husband and father with a grave kindness Cissy found appealing. His dark hair provided the perfect foil for Moira's porcelain complexion, sky-blue eyes, and silky red hair. As soon as Patsy McGinnis took over her carefully swaddled grandson, Desmond lifted his sister off her feet in an exuberant hug.

"Hey, we can even clear the ground now that junior's out in the world." He let her touch down gently and took inventory of her shining face before he reached for Cissy, blindly plucking her from the group as if he had special sensors that kept her in range automatically. He drew her to his side without taking his eyes off Moira's face. His intensity skewed Cissy's smile, but Moira's was as bright as her hair.

"I'm so glad to meet you." She said the words with such sincerity they sounded newly minted for this occasion and no other. All Cissy's misgivings evaporated at that moment. The exchange, indeed all they did and said the rest of the day, might have seemed commonplace, even banal, to an outsider, but to Cissy it was exactly what should have been done and said. There was a cookout, then a marathon softball game on the hard-packed sand left by the sea in retreat. Cissy played on Desmond's team, as did Moira, who was nowhere near as delicate as she looked.

When Patsy called Moira from the game to feed the baby, she turned to Cissy and said, "Keep me company, will you?"

Desmond noticed their defection and yelled loudly, "When you get the baby filled can we use him for first base?"

Laughter and rude noises nearly drowned Patsy's horrified, "Desmond McGinnis!" and Moira's fierce, "No, you can't!"

Inside, Cissy followed Moira to the deserted living room. She picked one of the inviting couches and handed the tiny bundle of life to Cissy to hold while she settled herself into the corner comfortably.

In spite of having two young nephews, Cissy had never held such a young baby. In fact, Moira's matter-of-fact behavior startled her. Iris rarely let even grandparents touch one of her babies, then only when she was hovering within reach, offering explicit directions. Sean Michael was only two weeks old, yet Cissy's arms instantly registered the impact of his moist warmth on her system. Within the confines of his blanket his tiny body throbbed with life. When her arms went around him he stretched his legs, then jackknifed sharply against her breasts.

Cissy gasped. His eyes were tightly closed as he groped with his mouth, rooting against her for sustenance, his face a living bud. Cissy was unprepared for the primitive surge of emotion that coursed her body, but Moira saw her reaction and understood.

"He gets to you, doesn't he?" she smiled.

Cissy looked at her wildly, wanting at once to rid herself of him at the same time she felt she would die if he were taken from her arms. She didn't know what to do, so she sat. He wasn't crying now, although he had been when Patsy had called Moira from the game. His face and the unruly thatch of his hair were the same tone of pinkish red.

"He looks like Des, I think," his mother said as calmly as if she had no idea that her words were exploding with terrible force inside Cissy. But Cissy was sure she did know.

She held the baby to Moira awkwardly. "He wants you," she said.

To make a liar of her, Sean protested with might and main, his thin, reedy voice breaking into a squall. Moira took her time opening her blouse, but finally she was ready and Cissy could sit back, relieved of her burden, yet strangely bereft. Was this awful emotion the maternal instinct she had been sure was missing from her makeup?

If Moira had asked her there for conversation, Cissy would be a disappointment. She was too shaken to make small talk. But somehow it was all right. Moira was as sensitive as the rest of the family, it seemed, and what she said could have been directed either to Cissy or to her nursing infant. Whether it was the maternal scene before her or the backwater feel of the quiet room within sound of so much activity that soothed her, Cissy didn't know, but after a while the effect was wonderfully refreshing to her ragged spirits.

By the time Sean had satisfied body and soul at his

mother's breast, Cissy and Moira were able to speak to each other like people who knew they would be good friends. Cissy was even composed enough to lift Sean away so Moira could dress and get to her feet for a stretch. When she reclaimed her sleeping son she grinned at Cissy and said, "He would make a pretty good first base now, don't you think?"

Cissy laughed, amazed that she could. "He's awful, isn't he?"

"Horrible," Moira concurred. "I'm going to take a nap now, too, Cissy. My eyelids weigh twenty pounds each. The only way I can keep up with this guy is to keep his hours."

"Can I help you?"

"You already have. If you hadn't been here, I'd have felt I was missing all the fun. Go back and hit a home run for our team."

But the game was over when Cissy got back to the beach. Surprised that something as commonplace as failing light could keep such intrepid players from their sport, Cissy stood on the deserted beach wondering what to do with herself. She needed time to herself, but the sudden loneliness was unbearable. She wanted Desmond. Where was he? Where was everyone? It didn't make sense that all those noisy people could have totally disappeared.

Reason told her someone would be in the kitchen, at least, but she walked away from the house down the silent beach. Not silent, she corrected herself. The tide still worried the sand, though from lower than she'd ever seen it, and gulls raced and squabbled at hand. Out in the channel one of the cruise ships, lighted like a floating cluster of stars, made its last run of the day from one of the off-cape islands. In her strangely distant mood that sign of human life only reinforced her sense of isolation.

She tried to think. Was this aloneness what she wanted? She wasn't antisocial, yet she felt overpowered at times in the bosom of Desmond's overflowing family. Wonderful as they were, wonderful as he was, sometimes she didn't know how to cope with what she felt. She was the problem. She didn't know how to merge with others and still keep her own boundaries intact. She wanted to merge though. Otherwise why would she feel so lost now?

Desmond had been right about Moira. Cissy envied her to the soles of her feet. And somehow it didn't help to know that happiness like Moira's was within her own grasp. She didn't doubt that Neil's love was the cornerstone of Moira's life, just as Desmond's was in hers. They loved each other. That was fact. But how could they build on that when she didn't know how to let go of all the pieces of herself and become half of a whole edifice?

Looking down for an instant, Cissy caught sight of a cluster of shells in the dark sand. She bent to investigate them, happy to be distracted from her tiresome thoughts. Behind her she sensed, rather than heard, another presence and turned.

She stood up. "Desmond?"

He walked to her without speaking.

She wanted to smile, but his seriousness alarmed her. "Why didn't you call to me?"

He stopped just out of reach. "I started to a hundred times, but you looked as if you wanted to be alone." His hands gripped the ends of a towel draped around his neck. "If you do, I'll go back," he said, his voice rough with emotion. "I kept telling myself I should, but I couldn't make myself do it."

163

She stepped forward with a relieved laugh. "Of course I don't want you to go back. I was looking for you." She touched his hands, tentative still in the face of his reserve.

"Down here on the deserted beach?"

Cissy closed her eyes briefly. He saw so clearly. "Not at first." She took a deep breath, determined to be as open as he was. "I was a bit overwhelmed by my encounter with your nephew and your sister, to be honest. I didn't see anyone about and I didn't feel up to making inquiries. I wandered this way. I was looking for you inside, thinking about you."

He unbent then, and let go of the towel to take her hands. "I've been berating myself the length of the beach for hounding you like this, but I couldn't seem to help it. I knew you wanted to be alone, but I couldn't let you go."

"But you did," she insisted. "You didn't intrude. I don't know how you learned to be so thoughtful, but you are. I wish I knew how to be as considerate of you as you are of me."

"That's easy. Just let me hold you."

She did, feeling a joyful sense of connection as his arms went around her slenderness. "I missed you." She felt the tremor of his body as if it were her own and lifted her face to kiss him.

"God, Cissy, I want you."

His mouth swallowed her response, but then he pulled away and held her at arm's length. "I swear this wasn't why I was dogging your steps. . . ."

"Please, Des, I feel the same way."

He waited no longer. Instantly he lifted her into his arms, carrying her with long strides to the rim of dry sand above them. He let her stand long enough to make a soft bed in the shelter of some rocks with his towel. His urgency thrilled her beyond anything in her life as he took off their clothes and came to her like a natural force, primitive and whole. She closed her eyes in bliss, finally complete. Her heart sang with the knowledge that their ability to merge like this, physically and emotionally in perfect oneness, had to mean they could find a way to blend the rest of their lives into harmony.

CHAPTER ELEVEN

Cissy started onto the porch, then stopped, frozen in the doorway, unable to move forward or to speak. She hadn't seen Desmond since their morning of clamdigging, but here he was stretched out on the glider, holding Sean propped against his thighs. With no one present but Sean she simply stood, drinking in the picture of Des bracing either side of Sean's tiny body with his big hands.

A baby Sean's age wasn't supposed to be able to focus his eyes yet, but Cissy knew Sean's rapt blue gaze was as fascinated as hers. He gravely studied the big man, testing the finger his uncle extended. His hand tightened over it and tugged it to his face. As Desmond's knuckle grazed his cheek Sean shut his eyes, groping to clamp his mouth over the joint. Desmond chuckled softly, "Sorry, old man, you've got a dry well there."

With perfect grace Sean let go and opened his eyes. Cissy was sure he was responding as she so often did to the gentle strength in Desmond's deep voice. Clearly he was both curious and content in this man's company.

Cissy had no idea how long she had been watching Desmond before she became aware that she was also being observed. She turned slowly and met eyes as blue as

Sean's set like jewels into the most interesting face she had ever seen. At Cissy's surprise the lined facial surface broke into a network of creases around a smile. The woman, who could only be Desmond's grandmother, beckoned for Cissy to follow her to the living room.

Nearly as tall as Cissy, she gave the impression of greater height by her erect carriage and the gracious tilt of her head. She sat down on the love seat and gestured to a facing chair. "You're Mary," she said simply.

"Mary?"

"Desmond told me your real name because I don't use nicknames." Her smile grew confiding. "I consider it one of the major triumphs of my life that Richard's name was never corrupted to Dick or Ricky."

"It must have been hard to enforce. I resist shortening Desmond."

"He told me and I knew right away I'd like you. I do, you know." She nodded toward the porch and added, "Especially after what I just saw."

Cissy's blush was deep and hot. "He's a beautiful baby."

Mrs. McGinnis laughed out loud at the attempted subterfuge. "They're both beautiful. As a grandmother I'm not supposed to have favorites, but if I do have one, it's Desmond. I wouldn't want to see him hurt."

Cissy couldn't think of a thing to say. Clearly she was being warned.

"As you saw, Desmond will make a wonderful father. Do you want children?"

"Mrs. McGinnis, I."

"Nana. Call me Nana."

"Please," Cissy choked, "I don't . . ."

Nana waved an imperious hand. "I know, I know. I'm an interfering old woman." The sparkle in her eyes told

Cissy she knew exactly how manipulative she was being. "It's one of the few pleasures left to my age. I can say what I choose and count on others to be more courteous." Then she sighed. "I apologize, Mary. My family lets me get away with too much. Especially today."

Cissy smiled, jumping on the chance to change the subject. "Happy birthday."

The hand waved again. "If men only knew how terribly attractive it makes them to women when they hold and play with small children they'd put women right out of the child-care business, don't you think?"

Cissy had to work to keep her mouth from dropping open.

"It's the contrast of size, I think," she mused. "Those big hands gently holding a small life. Desmond reminded me of Edmund with Richard and Geraldine just then." She got to her feet, surprising Cissy yet again.

As Cissy stood quickly, Nana patted her shoulder and turned away. "I'm glad we talked," she said over her shoulder. Was she crying? Cissy watched helplessly until she was alone, then she sat down, shaking her head.

"So this is where you're hiding," Desmond said from the door. He held Sean under his chin, his opened hands obscuring all but the baby's arms and legs. The force of Nana McGinnis's words returned. Naturally she had thought of her own husband when she saw Desmond with Sean. And of course she had cried. She was a woman still, as capable of being stirred as Cissy was.

Desmond came toward her. "Are you okay?"

Cissy sat up straighter and smiled. "Very much okay."

"Was Nana just here?"

"We were talking."

He grinned. "That explains the glazed look."

"She's remarkable."

"The poor man's Rose Kennedy."

"Desmond!" But she laughed. "You've been baby-sitting."

"I think he's been taking care of me, but he's sprung a leak, so maybe now I can return the favor."

"Don't let me stop you."

Desmond sighed. "The new woman. I bet my grandfather didn't get stuck like this."

"According to his wife he knew his way around the nursery pretty well," she answered, getting to her feet. She was embroidering what she'd heard, but it felt right to say it.

"Lord, she did get into it then, didn't she?"

"A bit. All in a good cause, I'm sure."

Sean's feet began to tattoo his chest. "If you say so." He dropped a kiss on her forehead and left her. She liked the way he didn't apologize or try to explain his grandmother. From the doorway she watched him take the stairs two at a time, admiring the blend of his care for Sean with his own manly ease.

Who am I kidding? she asked herself long after he was gone. *I love him. I admire and cherish everything about him. I'm already utterly and completely lost.*

Nothing changed her mind during the rest of the weekend. By the time she finished work on Tuesday she still had not broken free of her feeling that real life was the one she'd left behind with Desmond. The columns of figures she had pored over all day had been meaningless. What had a new issue of treasury bonds to do with life? Life was a wobbly neck trying to support a head of fuzzy red hair. Life was strong arms around her and a deep voice at her ear.

In her questioning mood the atmosphere of the gym seemed more pernicious than ever. She nearly turned at the door and bolted. Life was also outside, running grassy slopes under open sky, not cindered ovals below this cavernous steel-ribbed superstructure. The echoed voices and whistles sounded so eerie as she resolutely began her warm-up routine by the bleachers that she nearly missed hearing herself addressed. She blinked at Lucky. "I'm sorry. I didn't hear you."

"Come to my office." He turned abruptly on his heel, leaving her to follow slowly.

A sense of dread went with her to the cramped little room with the overflowing desk. She paused in the doorway while Lucky lowered himself to the swivel chair that shrieked in protest at his weight. Glossy photos curled away from the walls next to yellowed newspaper clippings. At least two she knew of featured her. She thought of emptying the straight-backed chair of sample running shoes and sweat shirts but decided against it. She knew she wouldn't be staying long enough to make it worth the effort.

"I'm letting you out of the program, Barlow," Lucky said without preamble. "You don't have it anymore. It's a waste of my time and yours to keep you on. I've given up trying to figure out what's wrong with you. Runners come back from all kinds of injuries worse than yours, but they do it because they work at it."

"I have worked, Lucky."

He sighed deeply. "I know you have. Sometimes, though, even work isn't enough." He thrust his hammy hand into his hair in the most affecting gesture Cissy had ever seen from him.

She looked away. She didn't want to like him now, of all times, and she certainly didn't want to feel sorry for him. She wanted to hate him. Instead, she felt only dead

170

and cold inside. She couldn't wait to get outside into the sunshine. "I'll clean out my locker and be gone."

Since that took very little time to accomplish, she got home long before Lorraine was due back from her job at the Boston University Law Library. Cissy stashed her duffel bag in the bedroom without unpacking it and paced the apartment. She needed to run. From the living room window she could see down Beacon Hill into the tops of the trees of Boston. The whole city was spread out before her. She could run in the Public Garden, around the Common, along the Charles River.

Only one thing stopped her. She still needed the proper surface, cinders or grass, until Dr. Ferris said her knee could take running on pavement. Dr. Ferris. He was the club's sports physician. Would he still treat her? He would tomorrow, she felt sure. It would be a while before Lucky notified him of the change, and by that time she'd have her checkup if she arranged it now. She could easily pay for it, that wasn't the problem; she simply wanted to be checked by the doctor who had treated her injury. Later perhaps she would find someone else. Later she wouldn't be a priority patient, but now she still was. The only appointment she could get, however, was a one o'clock cancellation. She took it.

That settled, she decided to expend her energy walking. She had the time and she was dressed for it. She'd shop. Have something to eat. Walk some more. By then she'd be tired enough to sleep, if she was lucky. Lucky. Lucky Edwards. No. She set off.

It was pushing eleven thirty before she returned home. She knew she was physically exhausted, but would her mind let her rest? That was the question. With any luck at all Lorraine would be out with Bill and she'd be able to make it straight to bed without having to talk to anyone.

171

But Lorraine was very much on hand. "Where on earth have you been?" she demanded before Cissy had the door shut behind her.

"I went to a movie."

"A movie?" Lorraine's voice slid up to the range of a dog whistle. "By yourself?"

"Why not?"

"Why not? Because Desmond's been looking for you, that's why not."

The logic of that escaped Cissy, so she shrugged and walked to the bedroom. Lorraine followed, five feet one inch of quivering indignation. "Don't you walk off on me, Cissy Barlow!" she raged. "When I got home from work Desmond was waiting in the hall. He went to the gym to meet you, only you'd left—without even running—and no one knew where you were. You weren't here and there was no note!"

She had no answer. Of course Desmond had come. Of course he was worried. She should have called him *and* left a note. But she hadn't. It was wrong, but there it was —done. She stared at Lorraine.

"Cissy, what happened? Are you all right?"

"I'm fine, but I'm really tired. I just want to go to sleep."

"Cissy, what is it? You're not fine at all. Did something happen at work?"

"Nothing happened at work. I went shopping, had supper, and went to a movie. Now I'm tired." She undressed swiftly and went to brush her teeth, shutting the bathroom door firmly on Lorraine's stew of sympathy and recrimination.

"Before you go to bed you'd better call Desmond, that's all I can say. I promised you would," Lorraine warned through the door. Cissy knew it was hardly her last word on the subject. She went straight to bed from the bathroom, and although she didn't sleep, she gave such a good imitation of it that Lorraine didn't disturb her when the phone rang. Cissy heard the rise and fall of Lorraine's voice, talking to Desmond undoubtedly, before she, too, came to bed.

She had no difficulty the next day getting time off for her appointment with Dr. Ferris because just before noon Warren told Cissy she no longer had a job with First Fiduciary. He explained what she already knew, that the job went with Lucky's program, that he had appointed someone else to take her place. The other shoe had dropped.

Because he was Warren Blaisdell and not Mr. Pritchard, he went beyond that announcement to explore her options as a runner and as a worker. He knew other coaches. He knew people in the business community. When she knew what she wanted to do he was ready to help. She cleaned out her desk and went to see Dr. Ferris.

She knew before she made the last turn on the stairs that Desmond would be waiting by the door. This time he had no book and no candy, just his briefcase and a look she couldn't read. She put down her briefcase and the shopping bag that contained the overflow from her desk to fish for her key.

"Don't you have to work today?"

"I took the afternoon off." He opened the door and helped carry her things inside. He hefted the shopping bag assessingly. "Did you go shopping again?"

Stung that he should think her reaction to stress sent her on shopping binges, she told the truth. "I was at the doctor's." Then at his look of concern she added, "For my knee. It's fine too."

"I'm glad something is."

Cissy faced him across the rubble of her career and took a deep breath. "I'm sorry about yesterday. It was rude not to call and—"

He exploded. "Rude! Cissy, rude is slurping coffee and forgetting to write thank-you letters. We're not talking about nice manners here. We're talking about feelings, about caring."

She started to defend herself, but knew from his expression it was useless. She shut her mouth and her eyes, determined to wait out the storm before she said another word.

"That's it, shut your eyes! Shut your mouth *and* your ears! Pull up the drawbridge and lock the gate while you're at it, but it won't do you a bit of good this time." His tone was deadly.

She sighed heavily and backed away from him. His anger beat at her in waves across the small space between them. "I said I'm sorry."

"Sorry! You don't know what sorry is."

So this was the temper he kept under such careful rein, she thought. She watched from within the remoteness of herself. She wasn't going to let him goad her into responding.

"Damn it, Cissy, you know I love you and yet when something bad happens in your life you crawl away into a hole somewhere without so much as a thought of sharing it with me. Do you think all I want is your body? Didn't you think I could help you? Or that I'd want to?"

"I didn't think that way! I was furious and hurt. I didn't even want to go to the gym anymore. I was going to break it off myself, for Pete's sake, but I didn't get to do it. He beat me to it. I was thinking about Lucky."

A look of understanding came to his face, and he said

slowly, "I just don't come into it at all, do I?" It wasn't really a question.

"Don't look at me like that, please." She couldn't stand the naked hurt in his eyes. "I'm not like you. I love you, but I don't know how to share myself the way you do. I'm hard inside. I really am that steel marshmallow you called me once. I don't know how to be what you want." She looked at him bleakly. "I didn't mean to hurt you."

His hands took her shoulders. "This hasn't gone quite the way I dreamed it, but I did hear you say you love me. I can forget the rest." His smile was thin.

"But it's the way I am," she insisted. "Desmond, yesterday I got kicked out of running. Today I lost my job. I don't know what I'm going to do. Loving you doesn't change that."

"It could." His eyes burned down into hers.

She couldn't get free. His hands were hurting her upper arms. "Desmond . . ."

"You could marry me." When she looked away, he demanded, "No, don't shut me out! Listen to me, Cissy. I love you. You know I was going to ask you to marry me. I want you with me. I wake up in the morning and want you there. It's the same at night and all the time in between. I can support you. You can run or work or do nothing. Just be with me and let me love you."

She began to cry. "You don't understand!" She shook her head wildly from side to side and his hands slowly fell away. "I can't do that. If you really loved me, you wouldn't even ask. You wouldn't put *more* pressure on me now. You know I don't want to get married."

Desmond straightened to his full height and stepped back. His right heel toppled her briefcase with a thump he didn't notice. It took him several seconds before he spoke and then it was in the coldest voice she'd ever heard. "You told me that a long time ago, but I forgot how vehement you were. I thought love would change your mind. I thought I could change your mind." Without taking his eyes from hers, he picked up his briefcase. He turned to the door then, his expression bitter. "I won't pressure you anymore."

CHAPTER TWELVE

The phone began ringing as Cissy unlocked the apartment door. She rubbed her sweatband over her eyes and leaned into the door. Common sense told her there was no chance the caller would be Desmond, but part of her never gave up hoping, even after four weeks and one day.

At her breathless hello Moira laughed. "You've been running."

"What else would I be doing?" she asked.

"Studying for your broker's license maybe?"

"Not on a day like this."

"It is gorgeous. I wish I could get out in it, too, but I'm swamped. Which is why I'm calling now." There was a note of apology in her voice, though calling was something she did with regularity that continued to surprise Cissy. She had never expected to hear from Moira, despite the fact that upon meeting her she'd felt an instant rapport between them. After all, she was Desmond's sister. If he wasn't involved with Cissy anymore, why should his sister be? But that wasn't the way she thought.

Cissy had been wary at first, suspecting the hand of a matchmaker behind what appeared to be a simple offer of friendship. Moira understood her suspicion and met it straight on. "My family doesn't dictate my life," she asserted. "I enjoy your company. I'll understand if you're not comfortable with me, but as far as I'm concerned this is just between the two of us. Even if I do think you and Des are perfect for each other, I'm not going to lift a finger to interfere. If there's one thing I learned being the middle child, it's to stay out of other people's business."

There were moments—too many of them—when Cissy regretted that Moira apparently meant every word of her pledge. She didn't pry or offer advice. She didn't even talk about Desmond. Though Cissy was starved for word of him, she was too proud to let Moira see how she felt.

"I'm glad you did call. Can I help?"

"I'm afraid you're going to regret asking that," Moira moaned. "I need a baby-sitter for tonight. I'd never ask you on a weekend, but I've run into some great social event that has the entire city of Belmont tied up, and Gwen is playing in a soccer game, Des is out of town, and Kev—"

"Say no more. What time do you need me? I can study there as well as here." She knew Moira had casually reassured her that she had no need to fear seeing Desmond and appreciated her thoughtfulness in spite of the stab of pain just his name sent through her. She heard out the directions and hung up, berating herself for not being able to break off even this small connection to Desmond in the interests of her own sanity. Without Moira to stir up memories, perhaps she'd be able to forget him and get on with her life.

She went to shower, arguing with herself. She *was* on with her life, Desmond or no Desmond. After the debacle of losing everything that structured her life in the space of two days, she had coped surprisingly well. Several things had helped.

Warren Blaisdell had immediately sent her to an interview with one of his friends in a brokerage firm. Like Warren, he was a sports fanatic who immediately saw her as an asset to his firm. Even without Lucky Edwards she was a local name in running. He saw the avid joggers and amateur runners of Boston as her natural customers once she had a broker's license to sell securities. Studying for that had given back structure to her jobless days.

The switch to outdoor running had helped too. Without a coach or track, Cissy had to design her own practice routines, set her own distances, and think about the goals she wanted to pursue. She'd gone back to the literature of her sport to study techniques and analyze her abilities. It had filled some of the hours left empty by Desmond.

The last thing that had helped her through her ordeal had been a delusion that Desmond wouldn't stay away. She hadn't known it as a delusion at the time; now she did. She had lived day to day with the hope that he would still want to be with her in spite of the way she had hurt him. His hurt had been based on a deep misunderstanding between them. He had seen his proposal as a solution to her problem of what to do with her life, and in another time, for another person, it might have been. But wouldn't he later have felt used by her? In his place she knew she would have.

Admittedly this was hindsight. She hadn't rejected him for that reason, but because in her state of panic marriage had looked like a bigger problem than the others to her. Now she wasn't sure that it was a problem, even to her.

She'd thought a lot about marriage since Desmond left. Now she believed she could handle it. She knew her goals better because of what she'd gone through, and now that the rest of her life was straightened out she felt as confident as it was possible for her to feel that she could marry Desmond and remain autonomous in all the ways that mattered to her.

She'd also looked at the marriages she knew best and, from her new perspective, found them vital. Moira and Neil's marriage was beautiful; even *her* family's marriages had improved recently. Both her father and Fletcher had become softer because of what they'd been through. Neither would have liked her term, she knew, but their easing and the stiffening of their wives had brought them closer as people and as mates. It heartened Cissy to see the changes. Probably she could see the good now because she wanted to see it. Perhaps it had always been there.

What she could still see, and never would forget, was the hurt in Desmond's eyes as he left. She ached for him almost as much as she did for herself. She had rejected marriage, not him, but that was a distinction he hadn't been able to appreciate then. She wanted to tell him, but she honestly didn't know how to do it. Could she call him? Go to his house?

All she knew was that her new life wasn't enough for her without Desmond. He had left a void within her that no amount of exercise, study, or achievement could fill.

Even without Moira to jog her memory of him she couldn't get through ten minutes without thinking about him. Maybe she could talk to Moira tonight. In spite of her neutrality, if Cissy asked her about Des, wouldn't she answer? Advise her?

The thought cheered her all the way to Belmont. Moira had promised that her baby-sitting skills would not be taxed by this session. Both of them knew Cissy knew little about babies. She enjoyed holding Sean and she could change a diaper, but that was really it. Moira was still the source of his food in spite of her hectic schedule of law classes. She would feed Sean before she left for her seminar tonight and when she returned Cissy planned to stay on while he nursed again so she could talk about Desmond.

That was the plan. Reality set in as soon as Moira left. She had fed him, she assured Cissy, but she left a bottle of orange juice just in case, warning as she left, "He seems a little fussy." Fussy soon turned to furious. Cissy walked Sean around the nursery and started to change a perfectly fine diaper before she put him back in his cradle and rocked him with soothing rubs on his back. He cried on. She left him alone for five of the longest minutes of her life, then tried again with the rubs and rocks. She wound up his musical toy. He outscreamed the tinkling sounds.

When she heard the doorbell she thought it was another chime from the wind-up dog until its persistence drew her to throw open the front door. If she wasn't prepared to see Desmond there—and she wasn't—he was even less prepared to see her.

They stared, gulped, and started to talk at the same time. Desmond turned on his heel then, and Cissy grabbed at his arm. "Please, don't go." She jerked her head toward the sounds from the nursery. "I don't know what's wrong with Sean. He's been crying like this since Moira left."

He took in her frantic face and followed her to Sean's side. He picked him up and propped him against his shoulder. There was no noticeable change in Sean's volume, but Cissy's relief knew no bounds. Desmond was holding him; everything would be all right.

"He doesn't need to be changed. I checked," she said over Sean's cries. "Moira fed him just before she left, so he can't be hungry." She was at the end of her checklist and desperate for something to say.

She felt as if she were all eyes. She soaked up every detail of his appearance, from his shiny brown shoes to his dark, coppery hair. He looked tired and thinner, or was she just being fanciful? Her heart turned over at the look of tender concern he gave Sean, remembering when he'd looked at her that way. He supported the baby's head securely and rubbed in firm circles low on his little back.

"He probably has a bubble." Sean turned toward the deep voice, offering the smallest of pauses between cries.

Cissy watched Desmond's hands, unable to look away. "I rubbed his back," she apologized, "but I probably didn't do it right."

Desmond smiled at her then. "Babies cry, Cissy. He'll live."

Tears stung in her eyes then and she turned away quickly. Fortunately Sean chose that moment to release a huge burp and their answering laughter saved her from discovery. Desmond continued soothing Sean, who continued to cry, though not with the same conviction. The process, as mesmerizing for Cissy as it was for the baby, raised another minor bubble before it put Sean to sleep. Cissy watched Desmond lower him to the cradle with a rising sense of panic.

Now what? How could she keep him from leaving? Could she keep herself from throwing herself into his arms? What if she cried? She turned away before he could see her face, her only coherent thought that she had to prevent him from going. She got to the nursery door before he did and sidled through it.

"You look tired. Let me make some coffee." It was all she could think to say as she placed herself strategically between him and the door. Was she going to tackle him if he tried to go? "Moira said you were out of town."

"Or you wouldn't be here." It wasn't quite the cold voice she hated, but it was flat and uninflected.

"Only in the obvious sense. No one who wasn't desperate would choose me to baby-sit." Her small smile died and she added, "I'm glad to see you, Desmond."

"You'd have been glad to see Attila the Hun just then."

She wrinkled her nose. If he could joke, didn't that mean . . . what? That he was real? That he was Des? Oh, yes. But what else did it mean? She didn't know, but she had to find out.

"Please don't go, Des. I've missed you." Afraid her words weren't enough, she plucked at his rolled-back shirtsleeve and tugged him toward the kitchen.

He took a chair and watched as she found cups and saucers and brought them to the table. "I wasn't aware that you came here," he said quietly.

She measured the instant coffee with great care. "Or *you* wouldn't be here." She looked up in time to see his reaction.

"No."

She sat down quickly. "No, you wouldn't be here? Or no, it wouldn't matter?"

"Cissy, I can't sit here and pretend it's not tearing me apart to see you. I wouldn't willingly do this to myself."

"I still love you."

"That was never the issue."

"I wanted to call you."

"To say what?"

She took a deep breath. "I didn't mean to hurt you. I wasn't rejecting you, just marriage."

"Semantics, Cissy. You were rejecting me because marriage is what I want. We're a package deal." He looked away from her face to the stove, where one unattended burner blazed. His mouth twisted into a lopsided grin. "Am I ever going to get that coffee?"

She jumped up, filled the teakettle, and placed it on the flame.

"Are you running now?" he asked.

"More than ever. I don't have a coach yet, but I'm talking to a couple of guys about marathons. Later in the winter I'm going to try to qualify for Boston. It will mean some traveling. My sprint was always my weakness in the shorter distances, but I have tons of stamina. I like the idea of doing something new. I was so stale until you helped me." She stared at the blue flames circling the copper-bottomed kettle. She had been babbling.

"You've lost more weight."

"But I eat like a horse. Even eggs now. You wouldn't know my refrigerator." The scream of the kettle rescued her from having to keep on talking. She poured the water and sat back at the table.

"No phony cream anymore?" he asked, gesturing to her black coffee.

"I'm not going to drink it. I just didn't want you to leave." Her frankness obviously startled him, but no more than it did her. She seemed to have no say in what came out of her mouth. To regain self-control she asked about his trip.

"We've been retooling factories right and left. I've been made a division manager, but until we can get some new people to take over some of the load I have to do double-duty."

"That explains why you look thinner." She pushed up from the table to see if Moira had anything to feed him. She didn't know the kitchen well, so her search took her into what turned out to be some unlikely cabinets. She turned when she finally found a plastic bag with some Oreo cookies in it to see him standing only a step or two behind her.

He glared at the cookies. "You're not going to be happy until you have me entirely out of my mind, are you?"

"I just . . ." She waved the cookies and took a step into his arms. "Oh, Des, I love you so much!"

She rose to meet the crushing descent of his mouth. It was a moment she had dreamed over and over, but now it was real. He was warm, solid and hard and here! His mouth pressed fiercely as his tongue reestablished claim to her sweet depths. She clung and pressed eagerly into his strength. In a blur she felt him break free to extract the bag of cookies she was crushing against his shoulder. He tossed it to the counter and pulled her against him fully. His hand followed the back of her plaid shirt into her jeans. His eyes laughed into hers. "There's room for my whole hand now, shrimp."

"There's room for all of you." She stirred under the warmth of his hand, then pressed her lips to his smile as his fingers curled up to find the elastic top of her bikinis and unfurled again next to her skin. She felt the remembered imprint of his body on her soul. "I need you so. Don't leave me again."

"Honey, that's something I could manage only once. I've been lost ever since you dragged me in the front door." His eyes were teasing and warm. "But we have to talk sometime." He kissed her, a biting little kiss that spun her head. "Later." Another kiss. He held her shoulders now and turned her away. "Go check on Sean."

Sean! She had totally forgotten him. With a frightened look over her shoulder she ran to his room and tiptoed to his cradle. He was deeply and sweetly asleep, one tiny fist clenched combatively by his nose. Relief and delight flooded through her, and after a few seconds she backed away to the door.

Desmond waited in the hall. He took her hand and pulled her into a bedroom. She looked around, seeing the thrown-back covers of the bed out of the corner of her eye.

"We can't . . ."

"It's the guest room. We can move in here if we want to." His fists rested on his hips in casual challenge that made her think of Sean.

She took a deep breath. "Des, I'll marry you, but . . ."

"I know you will."

Her eyes widened in surprise.

He picked her up and sat down on the bed, holding her in his lap. "I wasn't going to let you out of this bed until we got that settled if I had to keep you here a week."

She put her head against his, laughing to keep herself from tears. "I love you so, but I'm not good wife material. I have so many ambitions. I just can't be like your mother and mine."

"Cissy," he said severely. "Look at me. Follow my lips and listen for once in your life."

Surprised at his tone, she drew back to look at him.

"First of all, you underestimate your mother. Sure, she stayed home and took care of her family, but she's just as strong as you are. Second, you obviously don't know a thing about my mother or you'd never come out with such drivel."

"What about your mother?"

"My mother fit having five kids around running a real estate business with a gross take that would make your head whirl. She sleeps about four hours a night because that's all she needs. I don't know how she does it, but all your ambitions are nothing compared to what I've grown up with."

"But no one ever said—and she bakes cheesecake!"

Desmond roared with laughter and tossed her back onto the bed. "Dear God. The female mind." He landed beside her. "Yes, she makes cheesecake once in a blue moon and when she does we fall on it like starving peasants. Honey, where are your brains? By now you know what Moira's like. Whom did you think she got it from? I want you to be my wife, not my housekeeper. You can run all the way around the world if you want to."

She didn't get a chance to answer because he kissed her. She put her arms around him tightly, but before she could turn the kiss to her own advantage he pulled back again.

"But there is one condition to all this running of yours I want squared away," he began in a voice that instantly set her teeth on edge.

She watched his jaw set, thinking, *Oh, boy, here it comes. He is too good to be true. I knew it.*

"I know you need a certain amount of emotional and even physical space—more than I do—and I'll try to respect that, Cissy, but I will not be shut out by you. If you have a problem, I want to hear about it. I want to be part of your life, to share the bad as well as the good. So just get this straight right now, you've done your last running away from me. It's the one thing I'm through being patient about."

Threaded through his forceful words Cissy heard remnants of the anger that had sent him from her. She put her face to his shoulder. "You have been patient. I'm sorry you had to be. I'm probably never going to be as generous as you are, but I'm not the same anymore either. I need you. I found out how worthless everything else is without you, even my great ambitions."

"Why did you think I'd discourage your ambitions? I'm proud of them."

"I thought you wanted babies and a house."

"I do want babies and so do you. But we have time. We'll practice first." He kissed her cheek and brushed back her hair to find her ear. "It takes a lot of practice to make a great baby like Sean." He unbuttoned her shirt while she did the same for him. When he pulled it free of her jeans and began to kiss her breasts her hands faltered.

"See what I mean? I'm way ahead of you." He unzipped her jeans and released the snap with an evocative pop. Desire melted her to helplessness as he shucked her from her clothes and started on his own. "Just this once I'll help you though," he said in a voice heavy with emotion, "because I can't wait."

"Oh, my love, my love," she sighed. He told her how precious she was to him with every subtle caress and then with all the passion and strength of his body and soul, claiming and reclaiming her for all time.

Moira saw the kitchen and living room lights first, then Desmond's car by the curb, and, with relief, Cissy's car still next to the garage at the side. He had made it back on time as he had promised and the roof of the split-entrance Colonial was still in place.

She let herself in the door and listened to the quiet house. Almost quiet. Tiny snuffling sounds came from Sean as he stirred enough to set the cradle rocking gently. She lifted him from the bed and carried him past the closed bedroom doors to the living room. From the door she could see the two untouched cups of cold coffee on the kitchen table. Settling comfortably on the couch, she kissed Sean's damp forehead and whispered, "Just wait till you fall in love, my darling boy. It's so wonderful."

LOOK FOR NEXT MONTH'S
CANDLELIGHT ECSTASY ROMANCES®:

All-new

Candlelight Newsletter

An exceptional, *free* offer awaits readers of Dell's incomparable Candlelight Ecstasy and Supreme Romances.

Subscribe to our all-new CANDLELIGHT NEWSLETTER and you will receive—at absolutely no cost to you—exciting, exclusive information about today's finest romance novels and novelists. You'll be part of a select group to receive sneak previews of upcoming Candlelight Romances, well in advance of publication.

You'll also go behind the scenes to "meet" our Ecstasy and Supreme authors, learning firsthand where they get their ideas and how they made it to the top. News of author appearances and events will be detailed, as well. And contributions from the Candlelight editor will give you the inside scoop on how she makes her decisions about what to publish—and how *you* can try your hand at writing an Ecstasy or Supreme.

You'll find all this and more in Dell's CANDLELIGHT NEWSLETTER. And best of all, *it costs you nothing*. That's right! It's Dell's way of thanking our loyal Candlelight readers and of adding another dimension to your reading enjoyment.

Just fill out the coupon below, return it to us, and look forward to receiving the first of many CANDLELIGHT NEWSLETTERS—overflowing with the kind of excitement that only enhances our romances!

Return to: DELL PUBLISHING CO., INC.   B329A
       Candlelight Newsletter • Publicity Department
       245 East 47 Street • New York, N.Y. 10017

Name_____

Address_____

City_____

State_____ Zip_____

CANDLELIGHT Ecstasy Supreme

$2.50 each